PUFFIN BOOKS
MULLA NASRUDDIN

Sampurna Chattarji was born in Africa, grew up in Darjeeling, went to college in New Delhi and worked for seven years in advertising in Kolkata and Mumbai before becoming a full-time writer. Her collection of stories, *The Greatest Stories Ever Told*, and her translation of Sukumar Ray's poetry and prose, *Abol Tabol: The Nonsense World of Sukumar Ray*, are both available in Puffin. Her books for adults include a poetry collection, *Sight May Strike You Blind*, published by the Sahitya Akademi in 2007.

Other titles in the series:

MULLA
NASRUDDIN

SAMPURNA CHATTARJI

Illustrated by
Vishwajyoti Ghosh

PUFFIN BOOKS

PUFFIN BOOKS

USA | Canada | UK | Ireland | Australia
New Zealand | India | South Africa | China

Puffin Books is part of the Penguin Random House group of companies
whose addresses can be found at global.penguinrandomhouse.com

Published by Penguin Random House India Pvt. Ltd
7th Floor, Infinity Tower C, DLF Cyber City,
Gurgaon 122 002, Haryana, India

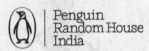

First published in Puffin by Penguin Books India 2008

16 15 14 13 12 11

ISBN 9780143330073

Typeset in Bembo and Century Gothic by Mantra Virtual Services, New Delhi

Printed at Repro Knowledgecast Limited, India

www.penguin.co.in

For anyone who shows signs of being a Seeker

THE

BOOK

OF

*MN

AND

**ME

*Mulla Nasruddin
** Shashank the Sad

Contents

Refuse to see things that simply aren't there

It all began with the turban. I was trying to get my Maths homework done when the turban appeared. At first I thought it was a curly bracket, but no, it was a turban.

'Shoo,' I said, 'stop distracting me.' You have no idea how distracting the appearance of a bodiless turban can be, that too in the middle of Maths homework.

The turban gave a little leap and vanished. (You have no idea how distracting a bodiless turban *disappearing* from the middle of Maths homework can be.) I spent the rest of the evening searching for it, and as a result my homework stayed unfinished and the teacher made a curly bracket of my ear the following day in class.

I decided that seeing things could only have one outcome—BAD. From that day on, I resolved, I would refuse to see things that simply weren't there.

Violent fists in the air

The next time it appeared, it had grown a beard. A neat beard, combed into a curly point, and floating above it, the turban. It was the same turban, no doubt about that.

'Oh no,' I groaned aloud, though secretly pleased, 'not again! Last time was bad enough. Go away, and come back when you're finished!'

The beard gave a little shake as if it were being tossed in the air by an invisible chin. The kind of action that would go with the old-fashioned sound governesses in English novels make when they say Hmmph!

'No, sir, hmmph to *you*,' I said to my Biology book, open on the page with the diagram of a heart. 'Can't you see I'm studying? Get off the left ventricle!'

It was just then that my mother popped her head in. Naturally, she thought it was unnatural for her son to be talking to his Bio book, so she rushed me to the doctor who pressed my chest very hard (I could have told him I wasn't talking with my chest) and said I was perfectly all right (I could have told him that too) and prescribed a daily dose of Sat Isabgol (which I thought was very humiliating).

'You wait!' I thought, making violent fists in the air at the non-existent turban, while gulping down the gloopy stuff. 'Just you wait!'

You can call me Al

Turned out, it was I who had to wait. The tricky turban
didn't show up for days. 'Scared you, didn't I,' I gloated, trying
not to sound too miserable. 'Serves you right! Twice bitten
once shy, etcetera.'

I might very well have started believing my own
pretences if it hadn't popped up—the turban, the beard and
a trailing rag where the feet belonging to the turban should
have been standing.

Not a rag, dodo, a rug.

I swear it, that's what the bodiless turban said. 'Not a
rag, dodo, a rug.' If I hadn't been downright bored
learning ancient Indian history and trying (in vain) to
remember those dates, I would have shut my ears and my
eyes once and for all. But who can resist a bodiless voice
rising from a page of Pallavas? That too a voice all rich and
roly-poly.

'What kind of rug?' I asked. Wouldn't hurt to be polite. He

was, after all, a guest (so what if he was uninvited *and* invisible).

A Persian rug, dum-dum. Don't you know anything?

I should have pulled the rug from under his feet and shown him the door. Uninvited, invisible AND rude. Instead I stared at what I now realized *was* really a rug, maybe even a carpet, with lovely intricate patterns. The invisible body was standing on what seemed like one end of the rug. Where was the other end? What was going on?

The doodle, for it looked like a doodle drawn in black ink, a fine black-ink pen, squiggled a bit and said, Well, aren't you going to say anything or do you expect me to do all the talking?

'I like that!' I snorted. 'When did you even give me a chance? Besides, don't you know good boys don't talk to strangers?'

And don't you know, and I doubt you would, just as I doubt that you're a good boy, that the more you talk to strangers the less strange they get?

'Oh go away,' I said, 'stop trying to tie me up in knots, I'm far too clever for that!'

Oh-ho! Clever and good! That calls for the rest of me to be here in person! Yes indeed!

And before I could say 'stop' or 'Sravanabelagola' or 'thingamajiggybob', two feet in curly shoes appeared and ballooning upwards and out of it came a body round and roly-poly like the disembodied voice, followed by hands sticking out of the sleeves of the robe, a little neck and then

a face with shiny eyes and a nose as sharp as the look in those eyes. The beard, which had been there all along, wagged happily, as if to welcome back the features it liked having around it.

Well, say hello, or is that something else good boys don't do?

'Hello, and stop calling me a good boy,' I said, wishing I could hide my delight at the final and full appearance of my disappearing doodle. Didn't want the man (at last I could stop calling him a 'turban') to get any more of a swollen head than he already seemed to have. 'I'm Shashank but you can call me Hank or Shanky or even S.'

In which case, you can call me Al.

'Al?' What sort of a name was that for this little guy with the turban?

Oh, never mind, just a popular song from my time. I guess you're too young to know it. Be done with niceties—I'm Nasruddin, Mulla Nasruddin, but you can call me Hodja, or what you will.

Mulla Nasruddin? I thought mullas were scary guys with guns. Not this little fellow with the wagging beard and eyes that hid a grin. But I know my manners.

'Nice to meet you, Mulla Nasruddin,' I said, 'I think I'll call you MN, if that's ok with you.'

Ok, S. Always did like the short form, the little guy, the one-liner.

And he twirled and preened a bit at the edge of the Persian carpet as if to demonstrate how short he himself was. Well,

I'm no giant either. One little guy to another. I felt like shaking his hand.

What was that you were muttering over anyway?

'History,' I said. 'Can't stand the stuff! All those dead kings. And dates dates dates.'

What's wrong with dates? Me, I love them. Why, only the other day I bought a handful of dates from that seller who claims to have the softest, juiciest dates in town. Keeps shouting how his prices are the best, as are his goods. So I asked him, 'Bro, what's so good about your prices?' 'All included, sir,' he tells me, 'no hidden costs.' So I buy those dates and I go home and I start eating them. My wife—yes, don't jump, I must confess I have one— is an observant woman. 'Mulla,' she says, for that's what she calls me, 'what's with the seeds? Can't you put them on a plate like a normal guy instead of putting them into your pocket? I'll have to wash out that pocket, not you.' 'Oh do stop fussing,' I said, 'I'm not going to throw away what I bought. All included, he said, so I paid not just for the dates but also for the seeds inside. Paid for with good money! If I like, I can keep them, if I like I can throw them away. For now I'd like to keep them. Happy?' And I went on eating the dates and keeping the seeds in my pocket!

MN looked triumphant after this little speech. I stared at

him. He was bonkers. What was he talking about? Dates? Seeds? What had that got to do with history?

Believe me, seedless dates are no fun...

And before I could blink, MN was gone.

It's funny, and I swear I'm not making this up, as I stared at the spot where MN had been standing two seconds ago, beard and rug and all, a line popped into my head:

SEEDLESS DATES ARE HISTORY.

I said it to myself twice, thrice and then I wrote it down. The more I looked at it, the more it made me want to laugh. He was right, seedless dates are no fun. From now on, I wouldn't be able to look at any date in history without thinking of seeds.

Can't you talk straight, like normal people?

Did that make my History homework easier? Well, I hate to say it, but in a way it might have. Every time I tried to mug up a date I would think of what was inside it—the event—and suddenly it didn't seem so difficult and idiotic as it used to. But you really don't want to know how I did my History homework, do you? Even I don't. So let me tell you that after the first introduction—if you could call it that—MN and I became thick pals. He wasn't like any other grown-up I knew. First thing, he never stood still for a second. Twirling, twisting, lying on his side, getting up again, clambering on to the top of my book cupboard, swinging on the curtains while he told me those crazy stories of his, he was as restless as my mom keeps telling me I am. And maybe I am, but that's only because my brain's buzzing all the time. When I'm chewing my nails or shaking my leg or tapping a pencil or drumming a table, it's because I'm thinking, thinking very hard.

Thinking about what? Everything.

But anyway, the second thing about MN was—he was so little! I sometimes felt like popping him into my school bag and taking him to class, but the clever guy never appeared in the mornings. And anyway I couldn't chase and catch him as if he were a lizard or something. He was my pal, so one day maybe I could just ask him to hop into my bag, nice and quiet.

'How old are you, MN?' I asked him the next time he landed up, knowing he wouldn't get offended like other grown-ups.

Oh, old as the hills, over the hills and far away, old man river—you get the idea. Do you know I once met Timur the Lame?

'Oh don't talk through your hat!' I said. I was in a bad mood. Don't ask me why.

Don't talk through your *turban* you mean, S. Try to be specific with words. What if you had to eat them?

'I'd never get that hungry!' I said. 'Now tell me about Timur the Lame.'

Aha, so the boy is interested! I could walk off, you know, and leave you hanging, but I won't because I like you. Once, Timur the Lame let loose his pet elephant in the fields of our village—

'Which village was that?' I said. I had been dying to ask

him where he lived, he seemed so well-travelled, and yet so at home in my little room in our Bombay flat.

The global village, dum-dum. Stop interrupting me. So this pet elephant, which was probably the only thing Timur the Lame loved, was wandering around freely, trampling the crops, eating up the grass, driving everybody nuts. But what could the poor farmers do? It was Timur the Lame's pet elephant, and lame or not, that man could shoot a mean arrow—nothing wrong with his eyes! So after a lot of arguing, they decided to go and ask him humbly to put the elephant somewhere else—like in a cage, perhaps, with thick iron bars? And who did they appoint as leader of the humble delegation? Yours truly! Naturally I agreed. You see Timur and I are old friends, I met him once in a Turkish bath, but that's another story. Remind me to tell it to you some day. Let's get back to the elephant.

We arrived at the court. I sent in my name and said I was there with a delegation. Impressive words are always useful in diplomatic matters, S. Old Timur agreed to see us in his reception-hall. And what a reception-hall! Gold everywhere, chandeliers, soldiers lining the walls with their sharp and shiny spears. The rest of the delegation—more like the rest of the mouse-pack—took one look at the sharp pointy spears and whoosh, off they went with their tails between their legs leaving me to face the madman alone. And he was mad that morning, hopping mad. His face was blood red and his eyes looked at me as if they'd like to burn me down.

'I haven't got all day, Nasruddin,' he barked, 'out with it!' 'Er, it's about your elephant, Sire,' I said, wishing I had run away with the rest, diplomacy be dashed. 'What about my elephant?' Timur barked, looking as if he'd like to bite my head off and chew on it. 'Nothing, Sire,' I said, blushing. 'It just seemed a little lonely, that's all. Perhaps you might like to find it, er, a wife?' and without waiting to hear his reply I took to my heels, wondering when I might feel a sharp pointy spear in my back. Now what do you think of that?

'You're a coward, that's what I think,' I said. 'Letting the poor villagers down. What happened to their crops?'

Who knows, by then I was in another country, trying to buy an elephant for myself. But where do I have the money to buy such a grand beast? So I go to this rich man and ask him to lend me some money. 'For what, Nasruddin?' he asks me. 'To buy an elephant,' I say, truthfully. 'You don't have money to buy it, how will you maintain it?' he asks, the stingy man. 'I came to you for money, sir,' I said, 'not advice!' and I left. Rich men are the stingiest, S.

Like the rich neighbour whose servant said he was not at home when I came asking for donations

to charity. 'That's fine, brother,' I said to the servant, 'But just give one word of free advice to your master when he returns. Next time he goes out he should not leave his face behind in the window—someone might be tempted to steal it!'

But then money does strange things to its owners or spenders. You know S, the first time I visited your country, I myself was under the spell of the few measly copper coins in my possession. I had walked a long long way and was desperately thirsty. If only I should come across a fruit-seller, I thought wishfully to myself. And lo and behold—I took a turn in the road and under a tree was a fruit-seller, his basket piled high with shiny red fruits! I gave him my last two copper coins and in return he gave me the whole basket and went off, having nothing more to sell. I was over the moon! This Hindustan is a very affordable place for a poor man, I thought to myself, and sitting down in the shade of the same tree, I started eating the fruit. The first one hurt my throat so badly I thought I had been stung by something poisonous. But still I ate, and ate. My throat burned, tears ran down my cheeks, my tongue was on fire and still I ate and ate. Just then a man walked past. Gasping and weeping I said to him, 'These must be the fruits of Shaitan!' The man laughed out loud. 'They're not fruits, Mulla,' he said. 'They're chillies. Stop! Why are you eating another one?' 'I'm not eating the chilli-fruits, my friend, I'm eating my money.'

'What? You were telling me about an elephant and now you're talking of chillies? What's going on? Can't you talk straight, like normal people?'

Oh don't be such a pest. Listen, I'll tell you where I went after the Timur episode—Kurdistan. Ever heard of it? That's where the Kurds live—or used to. Well, I travelled there to teach my teachings—which if you'll pardon my saying so—were much better than those of the pompous humbug holding forth in the teahouse back home. The humbug, a known pedant of those parts, was talking utter nonsense but so cleverly that no one could even guess they were being had. Anyway, so I decided to tell him about my travels through Kurdistan. S, what a country! What nice people! Wherever I went, they welcomed me with open arms—food, shelter, company, I lacked for nothing. And the public just hanging on to my every word! You can imagine Mr Pompous wasn't too pleased to hear of my popularity in that faraway land. He was losing his audience in the teahouse, you see. He said grumpily, 'So it was a breeze all the way, was it, Mulla?' 'Of course not,' I said, 'there was the time when I got beaten up, thrown into jail and then driven out of town.' Why they bothered putting me into jail when all they wanted was to throw me out again, I don't know.

You should have seen Mr Pompous gloat. But being a 'learned man' he couldn't show his glee openly. 'Why did they do that, Mulla?' he asked instead. 'Oh because they finally understood what I was saying.' 'And the people in the other towns didn't?' Mr Pompous asked, all puzzled. 'Well naturally not—in the other towns they spoke Kurdish, and I had been talking Turkish all the time.'

'You mean you went through Kurdistan speaking Turkish all the time?' I asked, marvelling at MN's cheek. 'What were you teaching anyway?'

Kurdish.

'What? You just said—'

I never said I didn't know any Kurdish, did I? I taught a chap all the Kurdish I knew. First thing I said to him was, the Kurdish word for 'hot soup' is 'aash'. 'Aash,' my student repeated after me. He was a keen sort of chap, so he asked, 'Mulla, what's the word for "cold soup"?' 'Oh there isn't any such word,' I said. 'The Kurds always drink their soup hot.'

I burst out laughing. MN was such a prankster. How did he get away with it? Well obviously he didn't get away with it all the time, otherwise they wouldn't have thrown him in jail. Poor MN. I imagined him in jail and felt terrible. Bars, a small cold room, no light. Slimy walls. Rats. Bad food. Mean jailors. Can't walk, run, play. Awful.

Why the long face, S? Now you're happy, now you're sad, blow hot, blow cold.

'Oh leave me alone, MN,' I said, angry at having been caught looking gloomy. 'I was just thinking—'

First mistake, buddy. Thinking gets you nowhere. Like that idiot who landed up at my mountain-house thinking he could learn something from me.

'Mountain-house?' I perked up. 'I thought you lived in a village?'

And who told you, my little city-slicker, that there aren't any villages in the mountains? Anyway, there I was in my house, or hut more like it, at the edge of a cliff. It was bitterly cold, S, and I only had this cotton robe on. I lit a fire in the fireplace but what a waste of wood. For all the warmth it gave me I might as well have lit a candle! Anyway, I was trying to warm my hands by blowing on them, when I heard a knock at the door. I opened it and there was this man with a silly smile on his face. 'Please Master Nasruddin,' he said. 'I have heard of your wisdom, and I thought I'd come and learn some of it from you.' 'All right,' I said. Who am I to try and stop a man from being foolish? If he'd travelled this far to such a cold place for a bit of wisdom, that was his problem. At least if he'd sat quietly while I finished warming my hands, I might have warmed to him. Instead he asked, 'Master, tell me, why do you blow on your hands?' 'To warm them,' I said, wanting to add, 'you idiot.' 'Oh,' he said, and became quiet. Just then my wife, having heard the stranger's voice, brought in two piping hot bowls of soup, god bless her. I picked up my bowl greedily—my wife makes the best soup in the world—and I started blowing on it. The idiot can't let this pass, can he? No, he has to ask, 'Master, *now* why are you blowing on your soup?' 'To cool it,' I said. With such an idiot for a pupil, my reputation would be shot to pieces. But I couldn't ask him to leave, that would be too rude. Luckily I didn't have to. The man left right after gobbling the soup.

'Leaving already?' I said. 'Yes. If a supposed wise man like you does exactly the same thing for exactly two opposite reasons, you must be mad. You're no master at all, I don't know what they were talking about. Sorry if I'm being too blunt.' 'Not at all, I sensed at once you were as blunt as an unsharpened knife,' I said and saw him out.

'And?'

And I went back to drinking my soup!

Thinking gets you nowhere

That night I kept thinking of something MN had said. Thinking gets you nowhere. Why did he say that? Thinking was everything to me. I thought all the time, about planets, about maps, about impossible missions and spacecraft, about the kind of car I'd buy when I was big, about accidents I saw on TV or on my way to school, about death, about my father.

I hadn't told MN about my father. But that's because we never talked about things like that. He just appeared, interfered in whatever I was reading or doing and went off on a tangent of his own. Actually, I liked that. I was sick of being asked questions every time someone came to our house, with a sad-weepy face. MN never asked me anything. But I would have liked to tell him.

My father was dead. He died in a train. Not of a heart attack or anything. A blast killed him. He was coming home as usual, except that day it wasn't as usual. There was a bomb in his train and it blasted the compartment to pieces.

I don't want to think about it.

Thinking gets you nowhere.

Maybe MN was right. What had thinking about the same thing over and over again got me? Certainly not my father back. Certainly not better marks in school. In fact my marks had got worse. And my mom kept panicking about me. Like the time she rushed me to the doc because I was speaking to MN—who was then only a turban. She thinks I'm going nuts. She thinks *she's* going nuts. She thinks—though she doesn't say it—that it's all her fault. She had asked Papa to come home early that day, she wanted the three of us to go out to buy some stuff for my birthday. Can't it wait till the weekend, Papa had said to her. No, Mummy had said, because Shashank's birthday is on the weekend, and so, laughing at himself for forgetting, Papa had agreed to come home early. Except he never came home at all. So now she blames herself, no matter how much Bua and the rest explain that it's not her fault.

Thinking gets you nowhere.

If wishes were horses

Have you ever wondered why camels don't have wings?

'What?' I was in the middle of a complicated quadratic and I had no idea MN had arrived.

Why camels don't have wings?

'How silly, why should they?' I said impatiently, though actually I was glad to have some excuse to lay my pen down, if only to quarrel with MN. 'They don't need wings, that's why. They need humps, to store water for those long desert journeys. Everyone knows that!'

But have you never wondered, why not wings?

Man, he was persistent! 'No,' I said. 'Anyway, you yourself said thinking is a mistake. Gets you nowhere. So why should I waste my time, that too thinking such nonsense?'

This isn't thinking, S! This is marvelling. At how perfect everything is, just as it should be, and all for our benefit!

'Whose benefit?'

Ours, you and me, mankind.

MN had obviously gone nuts. What was he harping about? Camels, wings, mankind.

'Why don't you just get to the point, MN,' I said, as patiently as I could. (I think I sounded like my mother does when she's talking to me.)

There *is* no point, except to marvel! Just imagine, if camels had wings—

'If wishes were horses, then beggars would ride,' I suddenly said. 'If turnips were watches, then I would have one. If "its" and "ans" were pots and pans, then I'd have plenty!'

Who knows where and when I learnt this rhyme, but it just came blurting out of me. I expected MN to be irritated at my butting in like that. But no, he was grinning from ear to ear, and his beard was doing its happy wiggle.

Exactly! Except if camels had wings, we'd be in serious trouble. No lucky beggars and watches and pans. Just imagine, if camels had wings they would be doing what those pigeons are doing outside your window. Hear them cooing and flapping their wings? Imagine a camel flapping its wings outside your window, trying to build a nest on that ledge, disturbing you with its spitting and chewing. Think of the damage it'd do! Roofs breaking, TV signals getting interrupted because a camel just flew past, all kinds of drama! No, S, life would be unnecessarily complicated if that happened and so, very wisely, camels were designed without wings!

'If camels had wings, life would be trouble, if they were dromedaries, it would be double.'

Bravo, S. You are a poet and I did not know it! Give me five!

I cheered up. MN was always good for my mood. Where did he get so much energy? What made him so happy? Sometimes I felt like I was the older of the two.

'MN,' I said. 'How old are you?'

Again? Why, what does it matter? Ok, I'll tell you. I'm three years older than my brother.

'So how old is your brother?'

He says he's two years younger than me.

'What? That means you're two years older than him, MN, not three!' I exclaimed, wanting to laugh at MN's lack of subtraction skills.

You haven't heard the whole story. That's what he said a year ago. I'm older now by one year. Therefore this year I'm three years older than my brother, next year I'll be four years older. At this rate it won't be long before he starts calling me granddad.

'That's nonsense!' I burst out laughing.

No, S, that's logic. Now listen, do you or do you not want to know what happened last night?

'Sure I do.'

I met this yogi and this priest. You know how it is, one decides to go on a long journey, meet some new people, find out how others live, make new friends, that kind of thing. Well, so there we were, the three of us, we became pally, and next thing you know, I'm deputized to collect money from the villagers for us to buy some food. The people were kind enough, a Sufi robe always makes them generous, and so when I rejoined my new friends I was happy, hungry and carrying the halwa I had bought with the money I'd collected. 'Let's eat, brothers,' I said to the yogi and the priest, but they weren't hungry and wanted to wait till night. 'All right,' I said, and we walked on. That's how it is with travelling companions—it's got to be one for all, all for one, like those three-musketeer-fellows. Anyway, when it looked dark enough to be considered night, I brought up the question of halwa again. You can't imagine, S, what it's like to carry something so yummy when your tummy is rumbling (yummy-tummy—guess I can be a poet too, no, S?). The smell of the halwa was enough to make even a full stomach go bananas, leave alone an empty one. Ghee and sugar and raisins, mmm. Anyway I suggested I dig in first, because after all it *was* my effort that got us the money that bought us the halwa. But the duo didn't seem to think so.

'I should be given preference on account of my seniority,' the priest said, 'I belong to an organization, we believe in rules, and order and hierarchy.' 'It's me, sirs,' said the yogi, 'who should get the lion's share. I eat only once in three days, today is that day and what I eat now will have to see me through till my next meal.' All this was getting a bit silly, so we finally decided to sleep on it. Whoever recounted the best dream in the morning would get to eat the halwa first. Well, morning rolls around, like all mornings. The priest says, 'I dreamt I was blessed by my God Almighty. That makes me most special.' 'Not so fast, bro', said the yogi. 'I dreamt I had attained nirvana!' 'And I,' said I, 'dreamt that the Sufi teacher Khidr appeared before me.' The other two waited expectantly. 'He said to me, "Nasruddin, eat the halwa at once!" So, I did.'

'You did?' I asked, not believing it.

Naturally! What else was there to do?

'Didn't they get really angry?'

What good would that do? The halwa was already gone!

And MN hummed happily to himself.

'You know, MN,' I said, 'sometimes I can't understand why you're telling me these stories, or even what the stories mean. What *do* they mean, MN?'

Ever heard the one about my donkey?

The man was nuts. I asked him a question, and he answered with another question.

'What donkey?' I said. 'I thought you travelled everywhere on that flying carpet of yours.' I was being sarcastic. What did he think I was—a child? Feeding me all these fairytales!

Flying carpet? Oh you mean this rug, which you so rudely called a rag when we first met. No such luck, S. It's either shank's mare or my dear old donkey.

'Shank's mare?'

The old legs, dum-dum. But when I'm in a hurry shank's mare won't do. So out comes my donkey and off we go. Sometimes the donkey's in such a tearing rush I have no idea where we're going. Once I fell off the silly animal. There were these little boys, you know the ones who stand around at street corners, playing tricks on passers-by, the little rascals. They saw me fall off my donkey and started laughing as if they had never seen anything funnier. Ha ha ho ho hee hee. I got up, brushed the dust off my robe and fixed them with a stern eye. 'Why are you boys laughing?' I asked. 'Ho ho because ha ha you fell off hee hee your donkey,' they said, clutching their sides and rolling around as if they had gone mad. 'And what, you little fools, makes you think I didn't have a reason for falling off. Eh?' And I got on my donkey and rode off, leaving them with their mouths hanging open.

'But—'

And that's not the half of it. I walked into the teahouse to find the regulars having this deep

philosophical discussion. 'Let's ask the Mulla a tricky philosophical question,' someone said. 'Nah!' someone else said. 'All he knows about is donkeys!' And that someone-else sniggered. 'Who says there's no philosophy in donkeys?' I said, determined not to let the poor beast down.

'In that case, Mulla, tell us which came first—the donkey or the nosebag?' 'That's hardly tricky,' I said. 'The nosebag!' 'That's nonsense!' the sniggerer declared. 'How can you say that?' I challenged him. 'Because—' and he faltered a bit. 'Because a donkey knows a nosebag when he sees it, but a nosebag can't recognize a donkey. That proves the donkey came first!' 'You seem awfully sure, young man,' I said. 'But have you ever asked a nosebag if it can or can't recognize a donkey?' and with the stunned silence as my greatest applause, I walked out of the teahouse.

'That's like which came first—the chicken or the egg,' I said. 'What a silly question!'

Yes, dear S, and you are wise enough to see it. But adults! Sometimes I wonder who's the real donkey.

'I know a few donkeys,' I said, seeing that MN had gone off into silent-mode. 'In my class.'

Undoubtedly.

'Like this guy who keeps borrowing my notes—'

Yes! That's it! If there's one thing I can't *stand* it's borrowing!

I jumped. I thought MN had switched off. And here he was pacing up and down and looking excited again.

There's this neighbour of mine, always borrowing. If it's not a length of rope, it's a clothes-line. If it's not a clothes-line, it's my donkey. Last time he came, I said no, I've already lent my donkey to someone else. Just then the silly animal brayed. 'How can that be, Mulla,' my neighbour said, 'I just heard your donkey bray!' 'Well,' I said, 'if you'd rather believe a donkey's word over mine, what can I say.' You should have seen him creep away!

'But MN,' I said, determined to get some facts out of him. 'No one travels by donkey any more. At least not in cities. And even in villages they have tractors and things—'

I fizzled out. What did I know about the way people lived in villages? What did I even know about the poor people in Bombay? And what did I know about donkeys? The only time I saw one was at a traffic signal once. It was a baby donkey and it was standing there looking lost. The policeman was directing the traffic all around it, and the next day Mummy showed me a picture of it in the paper, with the headline: DONKEY STRANDED AT ZEBRA CROSSING. I felt like laughing at the 'silly animal' as MN called it, but it was also pretty sad. Like seeing a camel or one of those big temple elephants walking in the middle of all the cars and buses. Once an elephant was killed by a double-decker bus. I saw it lying on its side, bleeding.

It's not how you travel, S, but why.

MN must have noticed my confusion, and was pretending he hadn't. That was good of him. I couldn't bear to think about the bleeding elephant.

'So why *do* you travel, MN?' I said.

Oh, the usual—itchy feet. It's not cushy you know, even when you think it will be. Like the time I stayed at an inn whose keeper had heard of my reputation. He kept bowing and scraping, saying things like, 'I am at your service, Mulla, anything you want, anything at all, at any time, just call and I'll be there. Yes sir, personally, at your service, to do your bidding!' So fine, I went to sleep and I woke up in the middle of the night, desperately thirsty. 'Innkeeper!' I called. I rang the bell next to my bed. I shouted, 'INNKEEPER!' No sign of the innkeeper or any of his servants. Finally I couldn't handle it anymore. I yelled, at the top of my voice, 'Fire! Fire!' You should have heard them run. Noise, chaos, hustle, bustle. The innkeeper rushed into my room with a pitcher of water in his hand, his hair on end, screaming, 'Where's the fire, Mulla, where?' I waited till he reached my bed. I opened my mouth, pointed at it, and said, 'Right here.'

And that's not the last of it. You end up doing strange things on your travels, just to get by. Like that time I was in Aleppo during the Crusades, guess what I ended up doing?

'What?' I said, itching to ask what the Crusades were.

Digging ditches, that's what. All around me the Christian armies busy crusading, and what do I do—I dig ditches. Luckily a rich merchant saw me and bought me for thirty dirhams. He took me home and next thing I know, he marries me off to his daughter. So one day we have this quarrel and she says to me, 'Don't forget my father bought you for thirty dirhams!' And I said, 'How can I forget? Those were good days—my life was my own. I worked hard, I got muscles from all that digging. Until your father came along and bought me. Net result—you gained a husband, and I lost everything, even my hard-earned muscles.'

'So you were a *slave*?' I asked, incredulous.

Aren't we all? But listen, Aleppo, Ethiopia, Mongolia—the most favourite of all my favourite trips was the time I visited the Great Pyramid.

'Egypt? Wow, how lucky!'

Well, the man who saw me up the tree didn't think so.

'What tree?'

The tree I was sitting in, sunning myself, listening to the birds sing.

'What birds?'

The birds in the tree I was sitting in, dum-dum! Don't tell me you're getting as soft-headed as the man who asked me what I was doing. 'Visiting the Great Pyramid,' I said. 'That's no pyramid!' he said, as if *I* was the fool. 'A pyramid is made of stone and has four faces meeting at a point. That's a tree!' 'I totally agree,' I said. 'But if you came up here you'd see what I mean—birds singing, a breeze blowing, the sun shining, flowers blooming—I don't think even the Great Pyramid could be finer!'

'You mean you preferred sitting in a *tree* to seeing the pyramids?' I was aghast.

Something like that.

'I think you're nuts.'

Well, actually, so do I!

And with that he was gone, leaving me more puzzled than ever.

Talking to a little guy in a turban

Have you been wondering why I sit in a room all the time talking to a little guy in a turban? I sometimes wonder the same myself. (Of course it wasn't really all the time, I only make it seem so, because that's all I write down in this book.) Naturally I did other things, went to school, played cricket, watched TV, played video games, read books. I was what my teachers loved to call an 'all-rounder'. Or I had been, until recently. Things haven't been the same recently. Maybe I sit in my room too much. Maybe homework is an excuse. Earlier, I used to finish it real fast and then go down to play till Papa came home and Mummy called me up for dinner. Nowadays, I don't feel like it. Nowadays I feel like writing down everything I feel, everything I think. I've always been good at writing—my stories won prizes in school, everyone wanted to copy my essays. But I didn't feel like writing stories anymore. I felt like writing dark things, sad things, and I was so afraid I actually might write them down that I started doodling when I should have been doing my diagrams, and I only talked when someone asked me something. If MN hadn't appeared out of the blue I don't know what would have happened. Where had he come from? Why did he never answer anything straight? Was he even a Mulla at all? Or was he a genie? I felt ashamed to think I had been talking to a genie, as if I were three years old instead of thirteen. He said he wore a Sufi robe, he said he had dug ditches and ridden donkeys and fooled people. Was he fooling me?

What was normal anyway?

I decided not to sit in my room for a few days. I did my homework in front of the TV, my books spread out all over the floor. I even went down to play but the rest of the gang acted funny, and I came up after doing a bit of fielding, which I never enjoyed much anyway. Mummy started looking at me when she thought I wouldn't notice. I guess she was checking to see if I was getting back to normal again. What was normal anyway? Nothing would ever be normal again, so why should sitting in my room and talking to a little guy in a turban be any more abnormal than anything else?

In any case he cheered me up.

That evening I sat in my room till dinner, then after dinner till bedtime, but no sign of MN. No sign at all.

He's a time-traveller

He was an explorer, I decided, when he failed to show up day after day after day. He calls himself a Mulla but really he's like old Amundsen and Peary (or that Indian guy who was on TV for having gone to both the North Pole and the South Pole on skis). MN was part of the tribe that kept jazzing off to the ends of the earth. But even as I said that, I couldn't help wanting to burst out laughing. MN at the North Pole in his robe and his slippers? He'd freeze, and blowing on his hands wouldn't help either!

No, I thought a few seconds later, he's a time-traveller. Look at the way he met Timur the Lame and is now meeting Shashank the Sad. That rug of his is a time machine, the sly guy, and he never told me about it. Trying to fool me with donkeys! Who knows what kind of robo-jet he actually rides. Mean and Nasty, that's what MN stood for. Mean and nasty for not sharing all his secrets with me when I—well, neither had I shared any secrets with him. But so what, he was older and he should have known better.

Time-travelling and robo-jetting it all over the planet while I was stuck in my little room in Bombay, with nowhere to go and nothing to look forward to.

Mean and Nasty. Malicious and Nefarious. Moronic and Neanderthal.

I felt better after calling MN all these names, and I spent the evening thinking of a whole lot more. (One hundred and ten to be precise.)

I'll make you famous

I missed Mean and Nasty so much that I started writing this. I wrote down everything he told me, how he arrived, what he said, what I said, and it was way better than writing essays for school. I enjoyed it so much I almost forgot it was revenge. 'Just you wait, MN!' I said, tossing imaginary horns and gnashing imaginary fangs (to remind myself that it was revenge), enjoying the gnashing and tossing. 'I'll make you famous and then you'll learn not to leave like that! Soon everyone will be talking of you digging ditches and climbing trees and you'll have me to thank for it!' And then because the pyramid story was the last one he told me, and because I couldn't invent any—this was truth, not fiction—I decided to make a map instead. I'd make a giant map of MN's travels filled with trails and historical interest and dangerous swamps. I had seen that kind of map in some of my favourite books. Now I'd put one in mine.

This idea cheered me up so much I almost felt like MN had just told me one of his loony stories.

They could imagine more because they knew less

Those who think maps are easy to make (and I mean make, not copy out of an Atlas or plot on a sheet of paper) should think again. The only useful thing they taught us in school was scale—otherwise you would be running out and buying rolls and rolls of paper just to fit those blasted mountains in. I decided my scale (1 cm: 100 km) and I began to draw. But drawing a mountain and marking a spot where MN's little hut might've been didn't make it a map, it made it a sketch. I threw down my pencil in disgust and that's when I remembered I had something that could help me. It was in the bookcase in our hall. I would have to take it out without Mummy noticing, or else she would start looking at me in that funny way again. I was in luck. Mummy was on the phone in her bedroom, the door was half-closed and I could tell she was crying, softly, but still crying, which meant someone had just heard about Papa and was calling, and making it all fresh and painful for her again. I wished people didn't keep calling to say how sorry they were. Why didn't they just think it in their minds, or send a little card or something? Why talk, talk, talk … But right now it was lucky for me, and so I walked up to the bookcase, opened the glass door and there it was on the lowest shelf—almost lost between a big coffee-table book on the Himalayas that Papa's office had given him on his promotion, and a big fat Tata Yellow Pages that no one ever used. I had forgotten it was so tiny. When I first saw it, it had seemed vast and wondrous. Now it was what it was—a little desk calendar with spiral binding and in ancient-type writing the words: Maps of the Ancient World. And below a picture of an ancient map and a drawing of a ship with sails, the words: 'A desktop calendar from the Huntington Library', and at the back under little stamp-sized pictures of the maps for all twelve months, the details of how much it cost ($14.95) and where it was from (Southern California) and some writing on how 'beautiful' and 'informative' the maps were, 'featuring all the major continents' as well as 'Java, the Persian Gulf, and Mexico'. Papa's friend from America had sent it some years ago. Papa had given it to me, and I had loved the drawings, turning the pages in all directions trying to make out each and every detail. And then I had forgotten about it, until now.

I had forgotten how small it was, and I had also forgotten how beautiful it was. Those ancient guys knew how to make maps! They were so different from what we saw in our Geography books. They showed not just names of places and rivers and green areas for forests and little compasses for directions, they put in all sorts of other stuff. The map of Russia showed three men standing and talking, all with funny hats and one with a rifle. The one of Western Europe showed tiny toy-like castles and men (or were they kings?) camping in tents. The one of the Tierra del Fuego had birds in the centre of the map, a family and some others trying to kill (with arrows and a spear) an ostrich. You could make up so many stories just looking at these old maps. From the new ones, all you could tell was how to get from Point A to Point B. How boring. Those days maybe they could imagine more because they knew less.

Well that worked for me as far as my knowledge of MN was concerned. All I knew of MN was what he had told me, and that too in no particular order, jumping from camels with wings to halwa. I'd start with camels (without wings). My map would be like these ancient ones, with little stories in them. Not my stories, but MN's stories, and through them you could figure out where he had travelled and whom he had met. So, camels. Camels meant desert, as did dates. And desert meant Arabia or Africa or India. I decided to do Arabia so I could put in nice palms, and oases and a caravanserai and maybe even Mecca which would be a nice touch as MN must surely have gone to Mecca. When he came back I would show him my handiwork and he would be so kicked to see himself in a map, he would never go off again without warning me, or better still, without taking me *with* him so I could make maps on the spot, like those old guys must have done in the days before we got Google.

It took me all evening to draw a palm tree, an oasis and a caravanserai meant to be Arabia and that too only in pencil.

Why can't you ever tell one story at a time?

The next day, as if the making of the first map (or rather the start of the making of the first map) had summoned him back out of the blue, MN appeared, nonchalantly swinging the wide sleeves of his robe.

'Oh, you!' I said, trying to sound disgusted. 'Just been around the world in eighty days I presume?' (I was being sarcastic).

And you are Doctor Livingstone, I presume?

'Oh stop fooling, MN!' I burst out. 'I'm not talking to you, going off for weeks without telling me. I thought you were my friend!'

Thank goodness I'm just a friend and not a relative or a relative's relative or a relative's friend! Did I tell you about the time a relative arrived from my village with a nice fat duck as a present? I was so happy to see him (and the nice fat duck) that we chatted and chatted until a delicious duck soup was ready (remember my wife the fantastic soup-maker?). We all ate it with relish and my relative went back home. All good. Until a few days later, a stranger turns up (empty-handed) and says he's the relative of the relative who brought me the duck. Naturally I felt I should treat him like my own, so my wife makes another delicious meal and we send him off happy.

A few days later another person turned up saying he was the relative of the relative of the relative who brought me the duck. A little tired now (my wife was beginning to give me dark looks) we served him a delicious, piping-hot meal of soup. This went on and on. When the next relative-of-a-relative-of-a-relative-ad-infinitum landed up, I went into the kitchen and came out with a bowl. Expecting soup the man took a large spoonful and spat it out. 'But it's just hot water!' he said, as if I had insulted him. 'No,' I said, 'this is the soup of the soup of the soup of the soup of the duck my relative brought!'

He was doing it again! Not answering my questions (not even giving me a chance to ask them), not asking if I had missed him, not saying sorry or hello, just plunging into a story as if into a swimming pool! My heart was rising, but I still had on my disgusted face, just for the record.

Besides, what do you mean weeks? Hardly been gone a couple of days!

'What?' This was too much. One thing I *did* know was how to look at a calendar—especially one that didn't have ancient maps to distract me. Besides, so many school days had gone by, so many evenings trying to play, I knew what I was talking about! How dare he—

And anyway, time—though you might not like to hear this just after that story about the relatives—is relative. Who says your time is the same as mine? It's like the time my wife was baking some bread. While she waited for the dough to rise, she sent me off to get some water. So I went off to the river and sat by its banks. Someone came along and asked me, 'What are you doing, Mulla?' And I said, 'I'm waiting for the dough to rise.' He thought I was mad, but I knew what I was doing by the river, I was waiting for the dough to rise, just as sure as my wife was back at home.

Then there was the time I was sitting at a crossroads where nothing was happening. A passer-by asked me, 'What are you waiting for, nothing ever happens here.' And I said, 'Yes, maybe not now, but when it *does* happen I may not be around, so I'm putting in my time while I can.' Or the time I got very restless sitting at home doing nothing, so my wife (I was getting on her nerves and she couldn't get anything done) told me to go for a walk. So I went. I walked for two days until I met someone walking in the direction I had come from. 'Will you do me a favour, my friend,' I asked him. 'When you reach my house, will you ask my wife if I have walked far enough?' Or the time that annoying borrowing neighbour of mine came to ask for the piece of rope that was lying in front of me. 'I can't lend it to you,' I said, 'I'm using it.' He looked at the rope lying on the ground and said, 'But I can see it lying on the ground in front of you!' 'Yes,' I said, 'that's its use'. 'I see,' he said sarcastically, 'and how long, pray, will you continue *using* it?' 'Until the time I feel like lending it,' I answered. Or the time—

'Stop!' I yelled. 'I get the point! You're like a fast train, no stops until you pull the chain! Why, MN, why can't you ever tell one story at a time, why does it have to be so many that I lose track and they all run into each other?'

Ah! Now there's a question I *do* have an answer to. It's a curse, or a spell or a prophecy—call it what you will. You see, when I was a boy like you in school—don't laugh, even I was a boy once and even I went to school—I kept talking so much my classmates hardly listened to what the teacher was saying. So one day the teacher got really angry and said, 'Nasruddin, from today every time you tell one of your silly stories, you will have to tell six more, and everyone will poke fun at you and laugh at your

silly stories which you will be unable to stop telling.'
And that's what happened, only of course it turned
out to be a boon instead of a curse, don't you think?
Forget *my* being unable to stop myself from telling
my own stories. Even those who *hear* them can't
stop telling them! And then they start telling them
everywhere, with no respect for copyright. They're
telling them on spaceships, they're telling them in
Chinese noodle-shops, they're telling them in
conference halls and chat rooms—

'Ok ok, I get the idea,' I butted in quickly. 'Seven
unstoppable stories at a time. You tell them so fast I can't
even keep count!'

I had stopped being angry or disgusted (or pretending
to be angry or disgusted). MN and me were jamming again,
and there was nothing I liked better.

They're even telling my stories in Turkish baths.

'Where you met Timur the Lame?' I asked, eager to hear
that story.

No, this was after. Or maybe before. It really
doesn't matter. What happened is, I was
completely wrecked by all my travels, my robe was
torn, I suppose I must have been stinking, who
knows. Anyway, what I needed most was a good
long bath. So I walked into this Turkish bathhouse,
dressed in my rags, and the attendant, a burly bare-
chested man, sneered at me and gave me the
worst towel he could find—the threads coming out,

almost as ragged as my robe—and a tiny flake of soap. I managed to have my bath, and when I left, I gave the burly attendant a gold coin. You should have seen his eyes pop, S! An eccentric millionaire, that's what he must have thought I was. The next day I arrived at the same bathhouse dressed in my best—a fine robe with gold embroidery, a pearl-encrusted turban, you name it. You should have seen Burly rush to wait on me! Ji huzoor, salaam namaste, he was laying it on thick and I let him. Hours later, bathed, oiled, massaged, no shortage of soap or oil or attention this time, I was on my way out. Burly was bent double, his palm out for what he hoped would be double-triple-quadruple last time's baksheesh. You should have seen his face, S, when I dropped the smallest copper coin into his extended palm. Shock, horror and disbelief are not near enough to describe that look. 'This is for last time,' I said to him, 'the gold coin was for this time!'

'Served him right!' I said. 'Just because you looked like a beggar, he treated you like one.'

Oh, appearances-reality—I'm used to being taken for a beggar. I remember the time they didn't let me into a banquet I had been invited to, just on account of my appearance, scruffy as always. I ran home, put on my best clothes, which to tell you the truth, S, are most uncomfortable, and sailed past the doorman, who failed to recognize me in my

finery. Seated with all the high-and-mighty glittering guests, I helped myself to the steaming rice and fragrant meats, but before eating I rubbed a bit on my sleeve. My neighbour looked at me as if I was an escapee from the nuthouse. 'What are you doing?' he asked. 'Oh just feeding the real guest at this table,' I said. 'You see, the doorman didn't let *me* in, he let in my robe, so I'm just giving the robe its due.'

'You know, MN,' I said, feeling a sudden bond with the little guy. 'You're really incredible. If only I could say things like that when people treat me badly.'

I was hoping he would say something like 'who treats you badly, can I help'. No one was treating me badly. Life was. I wanted to tell MN that, but I didn't want to sound like a crybaby or a girl. I was hoping *he'd* ask me so I didn't look like I was dying to tell him. But he didn't. He was on his own trip (as always).

Or if only donkeys could. They get treated worst of all you know, S. Either they get lost or they get stolen or they get beaten. And when they get lost you start worrying and when they get stolen you go to the police station. And then the police ask you silly questions like, 'Tell us how it happened.' If I knew how it happened it wouldn't have happened, would it?

And sometimes you get so tired of riding the same old donkey that you decide to sell it. I did that once with my little fellow. Took him to the bazaar and asked the auctioneer to sell him off. I stayed on just to see how little the poor beast would sell for, so imagine my surprise when the auctioneer opened the bid at five gold pieces! As the bidding began I realized the donkey was worth much more than even I had guessed. A good loyal sturdy animal, the auctioneer kept saying and I believed him. I joined the bid and soon I was outbidding everyone else. 'Yours, Mulla,' the auctioneer said, 'for forty gold pieces!' And so I paid forty gold pieces and took the donkey home, glad to have got such a good bargain.

'But MN!' I protested. 'You bought back your own donkey!'

Yes, it took an auctioneer to remind me of its worth. After that someone came wanting to buy my donkey from me. 'Wait, I'll ask him,' I said, and went into the shed where the beast brayed happily to see me. 'Sorry, bro,' I said, returning to the prospective buyer. 'He refuses to be bought by you.' 'But why?' said the man, angry at being rejected by a dumb animal. 'Because he says a life with you will only mean a sore back, battered hoofs and an empty stomach.' Smart donkey, that.

'Why do you love donkeys so much, MN,' I said. 'Every second story has a donkey in it.'

And why not? Sometimes you don't see the

wood for the trees on account of a donkey being tied to one of the trunks. Oh I know how it is to pull the wool over someone's eyes, especially when they don't know where to look. You know, S, I guess I shouldn't confess this to a person of your tender years, but I'm going to anyway. I used to be a smuggler.

'A smuggler? Never! Didn't you ever get caught?' It was hard to imagine MN as a dangerous smuggler, carrying illegal goods in the dead of night, evading check–posts, giving the police the slip and then hiding out in a jungle where no one could find him. For that kind of role you needed a different kind of personality—a big moustache, a big rifle, an AK-47...

Caught? Never, not once. Oh they used to check me all right as I passed those infernal check-posts. They'd ransack the packages I'd loaded on my donkeys' backs, they'd mess up the straw by poking their sticks into it, they'd look through every pot, pan and bundle. Nyet. Nicht. Nothing. And so, annoyed but unable to arrest me, they would let me go. I did this for years and I actually managed to make enough money for some poor thieves to come and steal from me. Years later, I met the same policeman who used to check my cargo so thoroughly. 'Tell me Nasruddin,' he said. 'I've retired from the police, I can't arrest you now, and besides I don't care any more. What were you smuggling those days when we were trying so hard to catch you?' 'Donkeys,' I said. 'I was smuggling donkeys.'

'Wow!' I said. 'You coolly smuggled donkeys in under their noses while they wasted time checking your bags! What idiots!'

Indeed. Well said, S. But I've been an idiot myself, more often than not. Once I was carrying this load of very fine glassware, a present for the wife. You know—or perhaps you don't yet—how women like pretty things. So I was taking this pretty present home to her when I dropped it. The fine glassware was now finely shattered. Immediately a crowd gathered. 'What's wrong with you people?' I said, angry with myself. 'Haven't you ever seen an idiot before?'

And yes, I've been made an ass more than once. A bunch of thieves once fooled me and my son—

'Your son?' MN had mentioned his wife many times, but this was the first time he talked of a son. MN had a son? What was his name, how old was he, why didn't he come with his dad to see me ... I was dying to ask all this, but you think old Chatterbox would let me? He was going on like the Rawalpindi Express!

We had been travelling the whole day and both of us and the donkey—sorry, can't help it, he's there again!—were very tired. It was one of those long lonely highways, night was already falling and I didn't want to be attacked by robbers. Just then my son, who has sharp eyes for his age, pointed out what looked like an abandoned monastery. 'Let's rest there, Abba,' he said and I agreed. When we got closer, however, we realized it wasn't abandoned after all. A group of dervishes were in there, dancing and chanting madly—

'Dervishes?'

Oh, Sufi mystics—they dance their way to enlightenment, never mind now, let me get on with the story. So I asked if we could spend the night in their company and they welcomed us heartily and invited me to join them. Naturally I agreed, who wouldn't. Soon I was dancing like a dervish—now you know where that saying comes from—and repeating the new chant the leader had just introduced, which was nonsensical, but who am I to question a mystic? So there I was dancing and yelling, 'I give you my donkey! I give you my donkey!' We danced faster and faster and faster until I lost consciousness and fell into what I hoped was deep enlightenment. When I woke up, the dervishes had gone—and so had my donkey. 'You fool!' I said to my son, cuffing him around the ears. 'Couldn't you have kept an eye on the donkey at least?' 'I did, Abba!' the poor boy replied. 'I saw the robbers untying our donkey'—for that's what they were, not dervishes at all—'and I ran to stop them but they said, listen to your father, and I did

and I heard you shouting *"I give you my donkey! I give you my donkey!"* So I thought you must have given it to them and I let them take it!'

'Did you have to walk all the way home then?' I said, thinking not so much of MN as of his son, walking endlessly in the hot sun on a long dusty highway, holding his father's hand. Was he small enough for MN to carry when his legs got really tired? Papa used to carry me when I was smaller, he—

Oh no, the King sent us home.

'The king? Which king?' I hated how MN never said anyone's name, as if it were all a big secret. The only name I'd squeezed out of him (or rather that had slipped out of him) was Timur the Lame.

Oh the King, the Grand Panjandrum, the Beastly Badshah—what does it matter, all birds of a feather. The important thing is that the King spoke to us, two lowly dust-covered travellers without even the dignifying presence of a donkey. When we reached home, naturally everyone wanted to know the highlights of our travel. 'Nothing much,' I said airily, 'except that the King spoke to me.' 'The King spoke to him!' everyone exclaimed worshipfully, and after repeating it many times as if it were a mystical chant, they went away to tell their wives and children that Mulla Nasruddin had been blessed by the King's speech. Only one idiot remained. 'What now?' I asked, 'I've said everything I had to.' 'No,' the simpleton said, 'you didn't say what the King said when he spoke to you.' 'Oh that,' I said. 'Come here.' The simpleton came closer to me and I whispered the King's words into his ear—

'GET OUT OF MY WAY!'

Too much fun

My map suffered.

I didn't. I was having too much fun writing everything down.

Why didn't I wake up one morning and find I could do magic?

You know, my favourite kind of book is where the hero goes off on a journey. He's not really a hero-hero, but a boy, or an orphan, or just an ordinary little guy. (Never thought of girl-heroes, who would, maybe, be just the same as the boys, only different.) And the hero doesn't even want to go on this journey—that's the funny part—he doesn't want to leave his comfy home (like Bilbo in The Hobbit or Frodo and Sam in The Lord of the Rings or Eragon in Eragon) and go tramping about the countryside with wolves and dragons to worry about. But he does it anyway, and he turns out to be not such an ordinary little guy after all. Of course you have heroes like Artemis Fowl who are clever and super-cool, with all those gadgets and things, but I prefer the ones who are a little more normal, you know, until great danger makes them realize how strong they can be. Like Spiderman or Harry Potter. Ordinary guys marked by sorrow, with a great but hidden power that they themselves have to discover. I'd have liked to be that kind of hero in a story. I was marked, I had a great sorrow, I was ordinary. So why didn't I wake up one morning and find I could climb walls or do magic or fight evil creatures with a glittering sword in my hand?

We would never forget

The next morning, Mummy announced we were leaving Bombay. She was going to help her sister in Delhi run her boutique. We would all stay together (Mausi was not married), Daadi would be happy to have me around and I would go to a nice new school, and make new friends.

I looked at her like she had gone mad. Leave Bombay? Leave this city that was my all-time favourite? I had been to Delhi on holiday. I hated it. No sea, first of all. Bombay *smelled* different. And second of all, I was *born* here, my whole life was here—my friends, my school, my favourite bhel-wala. What did she mean, leave Bombay? Why didn't she ask me first? Why did everyone do whatever *they* felt like? What about what I felt like? How come no one even bothered to *ask* if I wanted to go or not? I wasn't going. I wouldn't go.

She looked at me as if she might cry (I felt like crying too, I was so angry, I felt like crying and hitting someone or something). And she said what I knew she would say and what I didn't want to hear. She said how she wanted to leave Bombay forever because Papa was no longer here. She wanted never to have to ride the train again and be reminded of what happened. She never wanted to see another train in her life. She never wanted … and she burst out crying and I stood there feeling like it was all my fault. Again. What about all the other people whose fathers and mothers and brothers and sisters died in the same blast? Did they all run away from Bombay? They didn't. They stayed. They were sad but they stayed. Not everyone had relatives in other cities to run away to. Besides, who said being in Delhi would help us forget? We would never forget. I wanted to say all this but I couldn't, so I just stood there and watched her cry.

'We'll wait till the end of the term,' she said, later. 'You can't miss classes.'

I said nothing. All I knew was that I had enough time to make a plan. My plan.

That's the problem with questions

When MN appeared that evening, all rumpled and out of breath, I was staring at the wall in front of my desk. Or rather at the soft-board on the wall in front of my desk. At the map of Arabia (still in pencil and incomplete) on the soft-board on the wall in front of my desk.

'MN,' I said. 'Will you take me with you?'

I've only just arrived, S. Give a fellow a chance to breathe!

It was true, he was panting, and looked like he'd been running. I forced myself away from the sketch of a tent on the map, and asked, 'What's up, someone chasing you?'

No S, it's me chasing my voice.

'Meaning?'

When I called the aazaan this evening, my voice was in excellent shape. I don't think I've ever thrown my voice as far as I did today. So as soon as I finished the call to prayer I rushed down from the mosque and started running.

'Why?'

To see how far my voice had travelled.

'And?'

Well I'm here, aren't I?

'And where was the mosque?'

Oh a long long way away from here.

'MN, will you take me with you?'

Where?

'A long long way away from here.'

You don't look good, buddy.

'I don't feel good. You haven't answered my question.'

Haven't I? That's the problem with questions, they rarely get answered the way you want them to. It's like that farmer who asked me if his olive trees would bear fruit that year. 'Oh yes, they will,' I said. 'But how can you be so sure?' the farmer asked. 'Because I am,' I said. Off he went and off I went. That day I wanted to look for driftwood along the seashore. So I took my donkey and went wandering up and down the beach, when who should I meet but the farmer! 'What are you doing here, Mulla?' the farmer asked. 'Looking for driftwood,' I said. 'You're wasting your time, there isn't any, I've already looked.' 'Well I'll just keep looking anyway,' I said, and walked on. Late in the evening I was walking back, with not a single piece of driftwood to show for all the hours I had spent combing the beach, and who should hail me but the farmer. 'Mulla, I can't understand this. You are a man who knows for sure that my olives will bear fruit, why can't you use those same powers to tell if there's driftwood on the shore?' 'My powers, dear friend, tell me what *must* be, not what *may* be,' I said and walked on home.

Home. I had always thought home was here, in this city, in this building, in this house, in this room. And now all that would change unless I did something fast. If I left Papa's city (for he was a Bombay boy too) I would leave Papa in a way that would be even more final than knowing he was dead. But if that was my reason, why did I want to go with MN, who travelled who-knew-where, and not with Mummy to Delhi, whose location I could mark on a map, and whose roads I could already see in my mind and hate? Who was running away, Mummy or me?

Some questions are better left unasked. Like those guessing games people play. Picking up the phone and saying 'Guess who?' How stupid. Or that game Twenty Questions. Do you know it? Simply complicating what's simple. Like the man who wanted me to guess what he had in his pocket—

'Hey that's what Bilbo asked Gollum!' I was suddenly listening again. I had thought of Bilbo yesterday, and now MN was talking of riddles and guessing games. Could he read my mind?

Yes, except there it was a matter of life and

death, wasn't it? Nothing so grave in my case. I asked the man to give me a clue. He said, 'It's yellow and white inside, it's shaped like an egg and it looks like an egg.'

'That's no clue—he gave it all away!'

Yes, and no wonder I got the answer at once. It was a cake.

I was about to protest madly, like I always did when MN said something completely wrong, but I didn't. Appearances-reality. Like MN in his torn robes versus MN in his finery. Same man, different treatment. Why couldn't the egg-shaped thing have been a cake? Why should every riddle have only one answer?

The truth isn't simply the answer to a question, S. Like I told a bunch of Seekers once—and no, before you butt in again, not the Seekers in Quidditch—if they wanted the truth they'd have to pay for it. Why, they wanted to know, why should they pay for something like 'the truth'? Because, I told them, the scarcer something is, the more it costs.

Always questions and more questions. And if it isn't more questions, it's answers. 'Everything has an answer,' a monk announced once in the teashop where my friends and I meet. I wasn't going to let that pass! 'Really?' I said. 'But just the other day I was asked an unanswerable question by a learned man.' 'Ask me the same question and I'll answer it at once,' the monk said, eagerly. 'He

asked me—"Mulla, why are you creeping into my house through a window this late at night?"' Naturally, the monk didn't know. And truth be told, neither did I.

Or take the time I was caught by a gardener just as I was filling up my sack with lovely fresh vegetables. 'Excuse me, but what on earth are you doing in my vegetable patch?' the gardener asked. 'Oh nothing, just passing through, you see I was blown here by a very strong wind.' 'Oh really,' the gardener said. 'And who uprooted the vegetables, or is that too much to ask?' 'Oh no not at all. You see, the wind was so strong I had to grab at the vegetables in order to stop myself being blown away all the way to China.' 'Indeed! And who put them into that sack, pray?' 'That's exactly what *I* was wondering. And if you hadn't interrupted me, I might even have been able to tell you!' I said, sweetly.

You see, S, nobody's willing to wait, always rush rush rush. The owner of the house whose wall I once scaled was no different. I had barely lowered my ladder into his garden when he rushed up and accosted me, mid-step down the ladder. 'What are you doing in my garden?' he demanded. 'I'm ... er ... selling this ladder.' 'Don't you know a garden is no place to sell a ladder?' he said, lips quivering in superior indignation. 'And don't you know that a ladder can be sold anywhere?' I said. I hate silly questions and all theoretical questions are silly. Like this one—if a man falls off a roof, will he break his neck? How do I know? Though the fact is, S, I do know. That's why I hate that question so much.

I was walking peacefully down an alley when a man who was fixing his roof fell off and landed right on top of me. I cushioned his fall—that's easy to see from my ample girth—so he escaped without a scratch. But I? I landed in hospital with a broken neck. There I was with my neck in a cast looking like a mummy from Egypt unable to turn this way or that, while that man was undoubtedly back on his roof, whistling happily at his good fortune. My disciples, an earnest bunch, came to the hospital to see me.

'How are you, Master?' they asked. What a silly question to ask someone up to his neck in plaster. And then the most earnest of them all asked, 'What wisdom can one derive from this event, Master?' 'What *wisdom*?' I said, not believing my ears. 'You see me lying in front of you and you still ask what wisdom? Shun blind faith in cause and effect— that's what wisdom! *He* fell off the roof and *I* broke my neck—if that doesn't teach you, young man, the wisdom of avoiding theoretical questions, nothing will!' But poor things, they were all very young. It's the old philosophers and pontificators who really get my goat.

Like the Travelling Brainies who arrived in my town. They were like this rock band, S, doing their gig all over the country. They would set themselves up in a public spot—a town hall, a village square—and then ask the local wise men to answer a bunch of deep, philosophical questions. When they arrived in my town they were like the Top of the Pops—undisputed reigning champs. No one, however old or wise or learned, had managed to beat them in any debate. Now I'm neither old nor wise nor learned, but for some reason the governor called me and asked me to face the music. 'Perhaps you better talk to them first,' he said nervously, 'get to know their way of thinking and so on.' 'Not at all, Guv,' I said. 'The less I know about how they think, the better for me. Bring them on!'

The meeting was arranged in our largest hall—the crowd was huge. From all over the province men, women and children had gathered to see and hear the Travelling Brainies vs. Apna Mulla. The Big Three stood on one side, all impressive and grave, their arms folded, their brows furrowed, their spectacles shining. I stood quietly in front of them next to my donkey. 'Fire away, gents,' I said, trying to help them relax a bit. The first Brainy came forward.

'Where's the centre of the earth?' he asked, looking smug. 'Right there,' I said, 'where my donkey's right hoof is resting.' 'What? How can you prove it?' he sputtered. 'How can you disprove it?' I asked. He couldn't. Brainy No. 2 stepped up. 'How many stars are there in the sky?' 'What, another chestnut? Exactly as many as there are hairs in my donkey's coat. And—' for I could see Brainy No. 2 beginning to open his mouth to protest, 'anyone who doesn't believe me is free to count both.' Gulp. Two down, one to go. I could almost feel their sweaty palms! The third greybeard stepped forward. 'Tell me, Mulla,' he said, 'in how many ways can the human mind perceive the universe?' The crowd gasped. Surely this would be too much for their home-grown Mulla, meaning me! 'As many, sir,' I said politely, 'as there are hairs in your beard, which I am ready to demonstrate by plucking them out one by one, and—' here I allowed myself the luxury of a little triumph, 'they will be *exactly* the same number as the hairs in my donkey's coat which will give you the exact number of stars in the sky!' The crowd burst into laughter and loud applause. The Brainies did nothing of the sort. They went into a kind of football-huddle, and after much murmuring and muttering, they came up to me, shook my hand and offered themselves up as my disciples. Good sports, that much I can say. Good losers. Sometimes it's good to know how to lose.

'I hate losing!' I blurted out. I had lost my dad, I was

about to lose my best friends, my home, my city and now I
was slowly losing my patience. This could not go on. I
couldn't just keep sitting and listening to stories that poured
out of him like water. It was never seven unstoppable
stories—more like seventy times seven.

So do I, MN went on. Man, he was like the wind! Once
I was down on my knees on the pavement looking
for my cupboard keys, when a friendly passer-by
asked what had happened. 'I've lost my cupboard
keys,' I answered. 'I'll help you look for them!' he
said cheerily and got down on his knees beside me.
We looked over every inch of that pavement
before he asked me, 'By the way, where exactly
did you lose them, Mulla?' 'Inside the house,' I
answered. 'What? Then why are we looking for
them here?' the friendly passer-by said, not
sounding so friendly any more. 'I don't know about
you,' I said. 'But I'm looking here because the light's
a lot better.'

'MN,' I said. 'What would you do if you lost the most
precious thing in your life? No, not the most precious thing,
the most precious *everything* in your life?'

First thing I'd do is correct your grammar. Or at
least I would if I were that scholar who got into my
boat once.

'Your boat?' Boats, donkeys, rugs ... what was he, a
travelling salesman?

Yes, in those days I owned a boat and ferried people across the river—

(I didn't even bother asking him which river—he wouldn't tell me—it could be the Euphrates or the Nile or the Yangtze for all I cared.)

—when this serious-type asked to be taken across. 'Sure, sir,' I said, 'I is at your service.' 'What sort of language do you speak?' the serious-type said, getting into my boat with a disgusted look as if he was treading dirt. 'Haven't you learnt any grammar, a grown man like you?' 'No sir, me ain't,' I said happily, pulling at my oars. 'That's dreadful,' he said. 'You've wasted half your life!' I kept rowing. It was a wide river, S, and unpredictable. Serious Sir was muttering under his breath about bad education and atrocious sentence construction and appalling lack of vocabulary, when I noticed the river getting a bit agitated. Oh not on my behalf, no! There was a strong wind that whipped the waves and soon my little boat—a wooden canoe really—was being tossed about like the bit of wood that it was. Serious Sir stopped muttering and started looking around him. 'Sir knowing swimming?' I asked brightly. 'No! Why?' 'In that case, sir,' I said perfectly grammatically, 'you've wasted your whole life. We're drowning!'

And so was I, but what did MN care.

Why was I so scared?

In the old-fashioned storybooks that Papa calls—called—Classics, I would have packed a few things into a little bundle, hung it at the end of a stick and wandered off to the nearest crossroad where I would fall into the clutches of either a tattered rogue with an evil squint, or a well-dressed gentleman in a shiny carriage. And my life would be one series of adventures till I found the true home I had always been looking for. The boy in those story-books was—according to the drawings—thin, with hair over his eyes and no shoes on his feet. I was thin and my hair did sometimes get into my eyes but no way was I going to leave home without shoes. And no way could I walk out with a little bundle, or even a bag that wasn't my schoolbag. Running away was not as easy as the books made it seem. Not with Mummy keeping an eye on me and all the neighbours fully aware of the schedules of each of the kids in our building and the watchmen knowing just which bus picked which one of us up and what time we came back from school and even the istri-wala and the bhel-wala on our road calling out to me every time I passed, just, for no reason but to say hello. And what about my building friends, and the friends in the next building, and my Maths Miss who lived down the road and who I sometimes bumped into in the evenings when she was doing her shopping and didn't look like a teacher at all. How on earth could I slip past so many people without being seen, questioned, stopped? Besides, where would I go and how? I didn't want to run away from Bombay, but where in Bombay would I hide? It should have been the easiest thing to lose myself in the crowds of Bombay. Then why was I so scared?

There. I said it. I was scared. They always keep saying boys shouldn't cry and boys should be brave and boys this and boys that but that didn't mean boys didn't feel scared and feel like crying. And that didn't mean I was a sissy either. I wasn't. I was just sick and scared and sick of being scared.

Suddenly, I felt like throwing up.

Mummy saw me coming out of the bathroom and she rushed up to me and made me lie down and took my temperature and rushed to the phone and called up the doctor and rushed out to buy the medicines instead of just calling up the chemist to send them and looked so frightened that I wished I hadn't got a stupid fever that would slow everything down, everything.

A script I had never seen before

I was in bed for a week. The fever only lasted three days, but it felt like it lasted forever. After the fever had gone, I felt bored and restless lying in bed but Mummy wouldn't let me get up and I was so bored and so restless and so weak I couldn't do anything about it.

I dreamt of strange places I had never been to and when I was well again I forgot them all. All I remembered was that I had been riding a camel carrying these huge rolls of paper on which I was marking the names of all the places I passed through in a script I had never seen before.

I had missed so much schoolwork that week I had no time to make any plans once I got better. And I didn't even realize that MN hadn't come even *once* in all that time, and neither had I missed him.

A road at the top of the tree

Well enough for a spot of the old chitchat, S?

'No,' I said. 'Well enough but not free enough.'

Uh-oh, it seems we have a grouchy lad on our hands today!

'I'm not in your hands. Go away.'

But I've only just arrived, S! And I would have arrived barefoot if I hadn't acted in time. Imagine walking barefoot on gravel. Some might fall for it, but not me.

Barefoot? Was he reading my mind again? Rather, reading my mind the way it had been a week ago? Could anyone do that? Did thoughts stay the way they were in some secret hiding place where you could dip in and find them when you needed them? Had MN been dipping into my thought-store? Why was he talking of going barefoot?

It was those boys again, those rascally chimps. I saw them as I was walking down the road—in a suspicious huddle under the big banyan tree. They came up to me, and their spokesman said, 'We were wondering if you can climb this tree.' 'An excellent and fruitless bit of speculation, my child,' I said. 'And what was the result?' 'Half of us think you can climb it, the other half think you can't,' the boy said. 'Well I'll prove just which half is correct, right away,' I answered, always ready for a bit of sport, and I took off my slippers and got ready to climb the tree. But something about the boys alerted me to the real reason for their interest in my tree-climbing abilities, and I realized it wouldn't do to leave my slippers behind. Quick as a flash I picked them up and tucked them into my sash. The change of expression on those rascally faces gave them away at once! 'Why are you carrying your slippers into the tree?' the little spokesman asked, 'You won't need them up there!' 'And who says so?' I challenged, beginning to climb. 'What if I find a road at the top of the tree?'

A road at the top of the tree. How magical and wonderful that sounded. It was there in all the old stories, in the Magic Faraway Tree and Jack and the Beanstalk, stories I had read when I was little. I thought such stories were for kids, how come MN believed in them too?

'And was there a road?'

How else could I have got here?

'You mean it's that simple? You climb a tree, you find a

road and you travel thousands of miles, wherever you want to?' I was beginning to get angry again. He made it sound so easy while I was sitting and rotting trying to think of a plan that would help me avoid going to the one place in the world I didn't want to go.

I never said it was simple. All you young people, jumping to conclusions all the time. Do you know it takes eight hundred years to make a lawn look like velvet? I have it on the highest authority—a gardener, who was watering exactly such a lawn. 'Tell me the secret of this beautiful lawn,' I called out to him from top of the wall where I was sitting and observing him. 'Come down here, and I'll tell you,' he said. So I jumped down into the garden, landing on that beautiful cushiony velveteen lawn, and waited expectantly for the gardener to reveal his secret. 'It's elementary (I almost thought he'd call me "my dear Watson"),' he said, continuing to water the grass as he spoke. 'You plant the lawn with the finest grass, you remove any weeds that show up—and believe me lots will—you water it everyday, and you keep it nice and even by cutting the grass as soon as it grows above the required length.' 'Oh!' I said. 'I can do all that! But tell me, how long before I get a lawn as fine as yours?' 'About eight hundred years,' the gardener answered coolly. 'Well, in that case I think I prefer the view from my window just as it is—without a lawn!' I said and vaulted back across the wall. I was a lot younger then, S, a lot more agile. Those days, alas, are gone. I guess it won't be long before all my teeth and hair fall out. As it is, I couldn't eat a thing these last three days.

'Three whole days? But you must be ill, MN!' I said, remembering how I had lost my appetite when I had fever.

Oh no S, not at all. Nobody asked me to eat for three days, that's all.

I had to laugh. What else could I do?

At this rate I might even make that strange rumour I heard come true.

'What rumour?'

I was walking down the street when I heard the rumour that I was dead. I went home to the wife and I asked her, how can one tell if one is dead or alive. 'Don't be silly, Mulla,' she said. 'If you were dead your hands and feet would be ice-cold.' A few days later I was cutting firewood in the forest. It was the height of winter, S, so chilly that even the exercise of swinging the axe and chopping the wood wasn't enough to warm me. Suddenly I realized my hands and feet were freezing. My wife's words came back to me. 'My hands and feet are ice-cold. That means I must be dead. That means I must stop chopping wood. Dead people don't chop wood—unless they're in a horror movie.' Since this was no horror movie but my own life, I

dropped the axe and lay down on the cold ground. It was so quiet that I knew for certain I had died. And then I heard wolves baying and howling and my poor donkey braying at the top of his terrified voice.

I had forgotten about the poor creature! He was tied to a tree and the cruel wolves, their grey fur glittering with icicles, were attacking him with fangs as yellow as the moon. I raised my voice and yelled at them, 'Go ahead, you nasty cruel animals! Take full advantage of a dead man! If I hadn't suddenly dropped dead, do you think I would have allowed you to attack my poor donkey?'

If you imagine all your troubles will be over once you're dead, you couldn't be more wrong. Take the time I was sitting on a branch and cutting it when a passer-by looked up and said, 'Nasruddin, watch out, you're sitting on the wrong side of the saw, you'll fall down when you cut the branch.' 'Not on your life, friend,' I said, and went on cutting. Next thing I knew I'd landed with a huge crash on the ground along with the sawed-off branch. I rushed after the man who was obviously a seer, and said, 'You foresaw that I would fall off! Can you foresee when I will die?' 'No no, friend, I am no seer. I just saw what was in front of my eyes, I can't tell the future!' But I wasn't going to let him go so easily. I kept walking with him and badgering him, until finally the man lost his temper and said, 'Oh why don't you drop dead!' The seer had spoken. What else could I do? I lay down and died. My friends found me and put me in a coffin and started walking towards the cemetery. We came to a turning and they couldn't figure out whether to go left or right. They stood there arguing, one saying 'left', the other 'right'. I couldn't take it any more. I sat up and said, 'When I was still alive, it used to be left. Why don't you go that way and see if I'm right?'

Why was MN torturing me? Didn't he know I didn't want to talk about death or dead people? (How could he, I hadn't told him anything …) And that too mock-deaths, games, pranks, the kind that little kids play. What about real death, where no one ever came back, or spoke to their donkeys or sat up in their coffins? People came back from the dead only in fantasies (and horror movies). Or in stories like that of the sanjivani, and that too because they're not real people at all but gods, or related to gods, who have friends like Hanuman who can carry mountains in one hand to bring the life-saving herb just in time. And even in fantasies sometimes people died (look at Sirius Black), and the people closest to them wept and couldn't do a thing. Why was MN joking about such serious stuff?

Don't you wonder sometimes, S, why people always take themselves so seriously? There was this dervish once (a real one, not a robber) who was standing and shouting these terribly serious questions: Where do we come from? Where do we go? What is life all about? I said softly to myself, 'I don't know the answers, but isn't it obvious it's all rather dreadful?' A curious bystander overheard me and wanted to know what I meant. 'Just look at us,' I said. 'We're born crying and we die crying. Obviously there's something dreadful going on.' Even the little ones aren't free of this disease. Once when I was teaching in school, a little fellow stood up and said in his loud public-speaking voice, 'Teacher, what is the hardest thing to do—to conquer a kingdom; to have the power to conquer a kingdom and then choose not to; or to prevent someone else from conquering that kingdom?' My eyes popped and so did my ears. Where did these little fellows get their ideas? 'Child,' I said. 'I know something much harder than conquering a kingdom or not conquering a kingdom.' 'What's that, teacher?' the boy asked. 'My trying to make you see things for what they really are.'

Take those cases they used to bring before me when I was a magistrate. Once, two men rushed in and one accused the other of trying to bite his ear. 'No, magistrate-saab,' the accused said. 'I did no such thing—he tried to bite his own ear!' I told them to wait for me and I went into my chamber. I spent half an hour there and when I came out I had a big bruise on my forehead. My clerk asked me what happened and I said, 'I spent the last half-hour trying to bite my own ear. Every time I tried it, instead of biting my ear, I fell headlong onto the floor. That's how I got this bruise. Havaldar, examine the two men. If the complainant has a bruise on his forehead, he tried to bite his own ear and the accused is innocent. If the complainant doesn't have a bruise, the accused is the one who bit him.'

Then there was that woman who came to me, asking me to order her son to stop eating too much sugar. 'Come back in a week,' I told her. When she came back I postponed the case for another week. At the end of the second week, I was ready and I said to the little boy, 'I order you from this day henceforth to eat less sugar!' The mother was happy that I had at last made an official pronouncement which her son would (hopefully) obey, but also a little puzzled. 'Cadiji, why did you wait two whole weeks to say this? Could you not have told him on the very first day?' 'Yes I could have, if I wanted to be accused of the same crime as your boy. You see, I eat too much sugar too! I thought I could cut it down in a week, but it took me two weeks to eat less sugar, and only after seeing if I could do it, was I ready to order your son to do the same.'

Of course I wasn't always a magistrate, though

I thoroughly enjoyed being one. In fact, I once had to appear before a magistrate myself. It was my wife's fault. She'd been nagging me for days to go out and get myself a job. 'I can't, dear one,' I said, 'I'm working for the Top Man Himself, the One-and-Only Almighty-God, may His Name be praised!' 'That's all very well, Mulla,' she answered cuttingly, 'but I don't see your boss paying you any wages!' She's sharp, that wife of mine, and absolutely right. 'He hasn't paid me because I never asked him to,' I said. 'How about asking him right now?' she said. 'All right, I will,' I replied, and went into the garden, knelt down and prayed, 'Allah, give me a hundred gold pieces—that's how much you owe me for all the years I worked without a salary.' And what do you know—a bag containing one hundred gold pieces landed next to me with a thud! I thanked Allah and went in and gave the bag to my wife. 'Mulla!' she said. 'I never thought you were a saint, but now I know you are!'

Much happiness followed. I let my wife order all sorts of dainty treats and luxuries—Persian carpets, Chinese vases, Arabian nights—you name it. And every time I opened the door to let the deliverymen in, I noticed my neighbour, a very rich, very miserly man watching everything with his beady eyes. One day I opened the door—thinking the consignment of Turkish Delight had arrived—only to see the miser on my doorstep. 'Who do you think you're fooling?' he snarled. 'That money didn't come from heaven! I heard you making that ridiculous request and just to have some fun at your expense, I threw down a bag of my gold, and you, like a fool, thought it came from God. Give my money back at once!' Can you imagine his cheek? 'Nice try, skinflint,' I said to him. 'You must have seen me getting that bag of gold and now you want to lay your greedy paws on it. No way!' 'In that case, Mulla, I have no option but to take you to court at once.' 'Certainly,' I said, 'but I can't go dressed as I am—have you seen my robe? It's torn and patched all over. Do you think the magistrate will believe me when he sees me in my rags and you in your finery?' 'What do I care about appearances, I know I'm in the right. Here, wear my cloak on top of your robe.' And he handed me his embroidered cloak. 'Now come on!' he snapped. 'Not so fast, skinflint,' I said. 'I'm not walking while you ride regally on your horse. I'll have no chance to plead my case if I arrive dressed in such a fine cloak but trailing behind you on foot like a beggar. One look at me and the magistrate will think I'm a thief!' 'Oh you and your nonsense! Here, ride my horse. Now are you ready?' I jumped on to his horse, and we rode to the magistrate's court.

Skinflint accused me of stealing a bag with a

hundred gold pieces from him. 'What can you say in your defence?' the magistrate asked me. 'Simply this, sir, that my neighbour is insane.' 'And why do you say that?' 'He thinks everything I own is his! Forget the gold, if you ask him who owns this cloak I'm wearing or this horse I'm riding, he'll say they're his.' 'Let me test if what you're saying is true,' the magistrate said and turned to the miser. 'Tell me, whose horse is that man riding?' 'Mine!' the skinflint roared. 'And whose cloak is he wearing?' 'Mine!' the skinflint roared. 'Go home,' the magistrate said, wearily. 'This case is dismissed.'

No one knew everything, not even grown-ups

That night I lay on my bed looking at the big tree outside my window. Tiny green parrots came to the tree during the day, squawking and flapping their bright little wings. What a racket they made! Now everything was quiet, and the tree looked orange in the light of the street-lamp. Normally I closed the curtains so the light didn't get in my eyes, but tonight I wanted to look at the tree.

Who was to say there was no road at the top of that tree? How could anyone tell until they had climbed it and seen for themselves? Why did people, especially grown-ups, say things without checking if they were really true or not? They kept making grand statements as if they knew everything. But no one knew everything, not even grown-ups. MN was not that kind of grown-up. In fact he wasn't like *any* kind of grown-up. He was the kind who *climbed* a tree to look for a road, even if only to prove that it wasn't there. What was he trying to tell me? And all those stories about being dead simply because someone told him he was, what was *that* all about? That was like kids playing dead when they shot each other with toy guns. Pretending. But wasn't I, wasn't Mummy, weren't we both also pretending? Mummy packing my tiffin in the morning, me going to school, sitting in class, taking down notes, eating, studying, playing, sleeping—why did none of these things feel real? I might as well have been a zombie, the way I felt. And Mummy? What did she feel? Who knew how scared she was? Even grown-ups got scared, but very few were brave enough to admit it. MN was one of those few. He admitted being afraid, he admitted running away (like from Timur's court!), he was brave enough to be scared. Like that story he told me of the time the king invited him to go bear hunting with him. MN was petrified, but how could he say no? So he joined the king's party and after two days he came back and everyone asked him how the hunt had been. 'Excellent!' he said, beaming. 'And how many bears did you hunt?' they asked him. 'None!' MN said. 'In fact I didn't even *see* a single bear!' 'Then how can you say the hunt was excellent?' they asked him. 'For someone like me, not to see a single bear on a bear-hunt is exactly what makes it excellent!' MN said.

Or the other story he told me where the king, who was in a bad mood, suddenly demanded proof of MN's special powers. 'Tell me what you can see that I can't,' the king demanded, irritably. 'Isn't that what you seers are supposed to do? Come on now, hurry up. If you fail, it's off to the gallows with you!' And at once MN said, 'Sire, I see a wondrous golden bird in the sky, its feathers gleaming, and that's not all, deep in the ground on which we are standing, I see demons, their hides dripping with slime, their eyes red with evil intent!' 'My goodness, Mulla!' said the king who, however hard he looked at the sky or at the ground, could see neither bird nor demon. 'How did you manage that?' 'It's easy, Sire,' MN said. 'All you need is fear.'

I was afraid, but what did my fear show me? All I saw before me was darkness. And I wasn't MN, the wonderful MN who said he could see in the dark. When he told his friends this, they said, 'If you can see in the dark, then why do you carry a torch?' 'Why, to prevent people like you from bumping into me,' said MN. He had funny ideas about the dark. Like the time he announced that the moon was more important than the sun simply because at night you needed the light more! Or the time he peeped into a well and saw the moon shining in it. 'Uh-oh, better get *you* out of there before the world starts panicking,' he thought, and threw in a rope with a hook at the end of it to fish the moon out. The hook caught on a bumpy part of the well. 'Aha! Gotcha!' MN said and pulled so hard he fell flat on his back. And right there in the sky above him was the moon! 'Now, what would you have done without me?' MN said to the moon and lay there happily, admiring it. Or the time he announced to the people in a village he was passing through—'The air in your village is exactly the same as in mine.' When they asked how he knew that, he said, 'Because

I can see *exactly* the same number of stars from your village as I can see from my village.'

Nothing he said was scientific or logical the way we were taught in school, but in the weirdest way, why did he always make sense? In the beginning I felt like contradicting him, but nowadays I felt like stopping and wondering why he said the crazy things he did. Maybe there *was* no reason, maybe he just wanted to joggle the way I thought. The way I *thought* I should think. Maybe he was just being friendly. And god knows, I needed a friend, even if he was a little mad. No, *especially* if he was a little mad. MN was loony. Once, apparently, he ran through a town stark naked. 'What happened, Mulla?' everyone asked. And MN said, 'I was in such a hurry to get dressed that I forgot my clothes!' Another time he raced past on his donkey and his friends asked him, 'Why the hurry, Nasruddin?' And he said, 'Can't stop, I'm looking for my donkey!' Yet another time he woke up his wife in the middle of the night and asked her to get his specs. 'But why now, Mulla?' his wife said, as she sleepily (and crossly) got him his glasses. 'I'm having a wonderful dream, dear one, I want to make sure I see it absolutely clearly!'

He who is unafraid of Timur is unafraid of anything

That night I dreamt I was in Mongolia. It was horribly cold, but I didn't feel it because I was dressed in some kind of fur. I was covered from top to toe, and on my feet, instead of my usual sneakers or school shoes were these strange boots that looked like they had been made from some kind of bearskin. How weird my own feet looked! I was walking and there was a spear in my hand. I felt hungry and thirsty and all I could see in front of me was this vast snow-covered plain, the wind blowing the snow off the ground in a way that made it look like mist. I had been walking fast but suddenly my feet began dragging and I couldn't take another step, when right in front of me I saw a yurt. It was exactly the way I had seen in books—not the triangular-shaped tent that campers pitched or the wigwams that Red Indians used to live in—but sort of roundish like a mawa-cake. It was made of brightly coloured cloth and there seemed to be a light inside it. Without thinking, I went in and found myself in front of a man with a long moustache and a lame leg. At once I knew who it was.

'You're Timur the Lame, aren't you?' I said, forgetting to be frightened.

'And you're DEAD if you use that word again!'

I gulped. Chopped into mincemeat before I had a chance to say hello.

'Please sir, I'm sorry, but I didn't know,' I said, wondering what to do with my spear which I was afraid might poke him in the eye, the yurt being smaller than it looked from outside.

'Do you know your own name, at least?'

'Yes sir, it's Shashank. Shashank the Sad.'

'Already giving yourself titles, are you? A little grand for your size.'

I kept quiet. I was dying to ask for something to eat but how do you ask a man who has killed god knows how many people.

'And where have you sprung from, Shashank the Sad?'

'From my room sir, in my home in Bombay.'

'Bombay? Never heard of it. And how did you get here?'

'I don't know sir, I had gone to bed and—'

'You don't know much, do you?'

'I know who *you* are, sir.'

At this he relaxed a bit and stroked his long, thin, sharp black moustache.

'Well that's inevitable. After all, I *am* Timur the Tyrannical.'

'But—'

'Don't even think of saying it!'

I didn't. Let him call himself whatever he liked. All I wanted was some food.

'Please sir, Timur the Tyrannical, could I ask for a sip of water?'

A sip of water was hardly going to fill my growling stomach but at least it might put the right idea in his head.

'Timur the Tyrannical doesn't drink water! Here, have a sip of this, if you dare!'

And he threw a sort of sloshy bag at me. I almost dropped it while trying to keep the spear from swinging around madly.

'And for Timur's sake, put that spear down!'

I put it down in front of me and looked at the sloshy bag. There was a stopper at its mouth, and I felt terribly nervous about opening the stopper and spilling whatever was in the bag, forget about drinking from it. But I had to. T the T had challenged me. I opened the stopper, twisting it round and round and then I tried to lift it in a way that wouldn't make the whole thing collapse on top of me. I managed one tiny sip—and the hot liquid stung my nose and made my mouth burn. Tears came to my eyes and I hardly looked at T the T as I handed the bag back.

'Does Shashank the Sad feel happier now?'

I nodded. I felt like someone had stuck a flaming stick into my chest.

'Does the pup want a bone, eh?'

And he threw something else at me—a sort of stringy-looking piece of meat with the bone sticking out. It smelt funny. And I was angry he had called me a pup.

'I'm no pup, sir, I'm a boy and I don't like food being thrown at me.'

The minute I said it I knew I was finished. I had argued with Timur the Tyrannical, and he would chop off my head. Or just toss me out into the cold minus my furs and shoes. I would freeze to death and wolves would attack me because I didn't have a donkey to distract them. In the silence that followed, I could hear the wind howling and it sounded just like wolves.

And then T the T laughed. It was worse than wolves. He laughed and laughed and his face went pink then red then almost purple and he started wheezing and coughing and to stop himself he glugged some of that terrible liquid and wiped his mouth and looked at me with tears in his eyes.

'The pup barks! Next thing, the pup bites! Well done, boy. He who is unafraid of Timur is unafraid of anything. Come here and let us eat together like two men, instead of a man and his dog!'

And he laughed and wheezed and glugged some more.

I felt even more nervous sitting next to him than I had standing in front of him. At least then I had a chance of dashing out of the yurt if he got nasty. But he was tearing huge chunks of some strange-looking bread for me and there were better pieces of that funny-smelling meat which once you got used to wasn't bad at all, only very salty, and there was that liquid which I now had the courage to say no to, at which he laughed and patted me on the back so I choked.

'So how do you know so much about me, eh?' he said while I was choking.

'Oh … ergh … excuse me … read in the books …' and then I knew I had to ask, 'and also, sir, a friend of mine told me about you …'

'A friend? That's rare. What's this friend of yours called?'

'Mulla Nasruddin,' I said, hoping MN hadn't been lying through his teeth.

'Nasruddin?' T the T licked some meat off his moustache (he had an awfully pink tongue). 'Little guy in rags, always talking his turban off?'

'Yes sir,' I said with a leap in my heart. 'That's the one.' Joy made me babble. 'He said he met you once in a Turkish bath—but he never told me that story …'

T the T gave one of his terrifying laughs.

'Yes, by Timur, it *was* in a Turkish bath! The little fellow and I were sitting there in the steam room when I asked him to put a price on my costly golden belt—the one thing I never take off, be it in a Turkish bath or an English bathtub. He took one look at it and said, "Five gold pieces." Can you imagine his cheek—he always had cheek that little fellow—Timur's golden, jewel-encrusted belt worth five measly pieces of gold! "Oho," I said, "Five gold pieces for Timur's precious belt? In that case how many gold pieces for the person of Timur himself?" "Now that's another question," the little fellow said. "*That* is beyond value!"'

And har–har–har T the T started laughing again. I could see MN had made a good impression on him.

'Another time, we were camping in this place that grew the most delicious aubergines—'

'What's aubergines?' I said, without thinking.

T the T stopped mid-breath. *Now* he'd cut off my head. But no. He smirked and said, 'O brave boy of little brain, aubergines are a kind of vegetable, roundish, cylindricalish, deep-purplish on the outside—purple! the royal colour— and when you cut them open there's a tender white flesh that tastes heavenly roasted, fried or grilled …'

I could see T the T almost beginning to drool. 'I think they're called brinjals, sir, or eggplants.'

'I couldn't care less what you think. I'm talking of aubergines, the most delicious vegetable ever. "Don't you think they're the best vegetables in the world?" I asked Nasruddin. "Yes," he said at once, "they are." "I want to eat nothing but aubergines," I announced and I ate nothing but aubergines for the next five days. At the end of five days I couldn't stand the sight of those things. "Take them away," I shouted. "I hate aubergines! They're the worst vegetables in the world!" "Yes," agreed Nasruddin, "they are." "But just the other day you agreed when I said they were the best vegetables," I said. "That's because *you're* my master, Timur, not the aubergine!" he said. Har–har–har–har!'

I was actually beginning to enjoy this cosy session when, suddenly, a pack of wolves filled the yurt with its howling, big grey beasts snapping at our hands and feet, snatching at the meat and jumping up to tear at our faces as we tried to fend them off. 'Run, brave boy of little brain!' T shouted. 'Timur the Tyrannical will single-handedly put an end to this pack of thieves! Run, and if you see that rascal Nasruddin, give him my love!'

And the last thing I saw before I woke up was old T the T slashing away at the wolves with the spear I had left behind in his yurt.

Mulla Nasruddin's Guide to Seeing
the World

'I met Timur the Lame last night,' I said casually to MN the next evening.

Oh? And I met Don Quixote.

'He sent his love,' I said.

Who?

'Timur the Lame, only he prefers being called Timur the Tyrannical. He called me brave boy of little brain, which isn't very nice (except for the brave part) and also not very original. It's Pooh who's the bear of little brain.'

I didn't know the old man had literary leanings. As far as I know the only thing he can read are cards. Next thing he'll be calling you the Knight of the Mournful Countenance as Sancho called Quixote.

'He wouldn't have to,' I said. 'I gave myself a name before he could!'

Ah?

'Shashank the Sad!'

Well, that's another way of saying the same thing, isn't it? Except you boys wouldn't be caught dead using big words.

'What do you mean?' I was a bit annoyed at how coolly MN took any news I shared with him.

Would you have called yourself Shashank of the Mournful Countenance?

'No, it sounds too old-fashioned.'

That's exactly what I mean. But never mind, a rose by any other name and so on. Surely the name Don Quixote rings a bell?

'Yes, he was the guy who went around fighting windmills on a donkey. Sounds a bit like you.'

I take that as a compliment. But I must correct you—he only rode the donkey when his poor steed Rocinante was too injured to carry him. It was his trusty squire Sancho Panza who rode the donkey, which they also called an ass.

'A donkey by any other name is still a donkey,' I said glumly.

And so it is, but that's no reason to pull such a long face, unless you're trying to fit the face to the name. Like trying to cut the coat according to the cloth, or some such thing. Talking of coats, Don Quixote was wearing a really strange vest, which he insisted was a coat of armour. And a basin on his head for a helmet! He's quite mad, you know.

'As mad as you?'

Oh madder, I suspect. And so delightful. A thousand thanks to Cid Hamete Benengeli for writing it all down.

'Writing *what* down?' Today MN was weirder than ever. And what was with all these names he kept bringing up? Who was Cid whatever-whatever-whatever?

The Chronicles of Don Quixote, of course! Don't you boys learn *anything* in school? Besides, weren't you planning a journey? Never plan a journey without a copy of Don Quixote under your arm.

'What journey? Who told you?' For a second I panicked. MN had guessed, maybe Mummy had guessed too. Maybe I had been talking in my sleep. Maybe—

You told me, S. And I told you you'd have to go alone.

When had this conversation happened? True I had asked him (foolishly) to take me with him, but in return all he had told me was a series of stories involving olives and driftwood and cupboard keys.

Travelling alone is better than travelling with friends. Once, a friend and I stopped at a café for a drink. We had been walking for a while and were very thirsty. Seeing the measly state of our funds, we decided to share a glass of milk. Don't make a face, there's nothing like a glass of cold milk on a hot day. Especially if you've got a bit of sugar to sweeten it with. We didn't have money for sugar, but my friend turned out to be more resourceful than I thought. 'I've got a bit of sugar here in my bag,' he said. 'Just one spoon. You drink your half of the milk and then I'll add the sugar to my half.' 'Why don't you add it now,' I suggested. 'One spoon is enough to sweeten this glass for both of us, and I promise I'll still drink only half!' 'No,' my friend said. 'It's not enough for the whole glass. Hurry and drink up!' 'Wait a second,' I said. 'I'll just be back.' I left my friend at the table, gazing greedily at the glass of milk, his little packet of sugar ready in his hand. 'You know what?' I asked, sitting down again. 'I *will* have my share first, as you suggested, but guess what? I'm going to have mine with salt.' 'Salt?' My friend turned green. 'Yes,' I said happily. 'So nice of the café owner—he's given me two spoonfuls, enough for the whole glass, don't you think? Cheers!'

'Ewww, and you drank it?' I said. 'How disgusting!'

That's what my friend thought. Anyway, then there's the question of weather.

'Weather?'

Yes. Travel in winter and you'll complain it's too cold, travel in summer and it's too hot, travel in the monsoon and it's too wet. Why doesn't anyone think of travelling in spring, when there's nothing to complain about? People like complaining, that's why! If it isn't the weather they're cribbing about, it's about how some people can stay dry in the rain.

'Like who?' I was feeling aggressive again. Dry in the rain! MN had obviously never experienced a Bombay monsoon!

Like yours truly, of course. There was this rich man who once asked me to go hunting with him—

'Hunting? I thought you were terrified of hunting.'

Only if it's bears. This man was hunting foxes, I think. Barbaric custom. Anyway, so he insisted I join his party and just to pull a fast one on me, he gave me his slowest horse. Everyone sped away and there I was, ambling along on a horse that, come to think of it, was a lot like Don Quixote's—slow, thin, tired—in other words, a hack. Just then it began to rain. No sign of cover anywhere and even if there had been, my Rocinante would have been of no use. So I decided to do the next best thing. I took off all my clothes, folded them up, sat down on the little pile they made and held Rocinante's saddle over my head. When the rain stopped, I put the saddle back, got off the little pile and wore my clothes, which were, as I had suspected, quite dry. I headed back, leading Rocinante by the reins. Poor beast, I didn't have the heart to ride him, and anyway walking was faster. Lunch was being served when I reached my host's house, and you can imagine their amazement when they walked in dripping wet, and saw me already there, dry as a feather boa. 'How did you manage it?' my host asked me. 'Oh it was that wonderful horse you gave me to ride,' I said.

The next morning, my host took the hack for himself and gave me the fast horse he had been riding. Fair enough. We set off and I was racing along when it started raining again. I quickly got off my Lightning Flash, and did exactly what I had done the previous day. My host, bless his heart, got even wetter riding poor old Rocinante back. 'It's all your fault,' he shouted when he walked in, soaked to the bone. 'You made me ride that awful slowcoach!' 'But I rode it yesterday,' I said quietly. 'Has it ever occurred to you that the fault may be yours rather than the horse's? Perhaps you didn't apply *yourself* to the question of how to keep dry in the rain?' Blame the rain, blame the horse, blame everyone but yourself! Blame is a funny game, S.

Once, some thieves visited our house when my wife and I were out. When we came back they had gone off with everything we possessed, which, truth be told, wasn't much, and proves just how desperate the thieves must have been. But anyway, seeing her beloved pots and pans gone, the wife started scolding me. 'You're to blame for not locking the door properly!' she said. The neighbours arrived, wanting to make the most of our marital squabble and misfortune. Yes, Mulla, she's right! You should have locked the door! You should have checked the lock! What are you saying, you should have *changed* the lock! Accusations poured in left, right and centre. 'Oh,' I said, 'so I'm to blame for everything, is it?' 'Yes,' they said, 'who else can we blame but you for the fact that all your household goods have been stolen?' 'Well,' I said. 'How about blaming the thieves?'

Speaking of thieves, some of them are truly shameless. I was at home once when a thief came in and carted everything away, leaving only the rug I was napping on. I got up and followed him. He walked into his own house and I entered behind him, rolled out my rug (which I had brought with me) and lay down. 'Hello?' said the thief, very annoyed. 'And what do you think you're doing?' 'Oh pardon me,' I said. 'I thought we were shifting house.'

But back to questions of travel. There'll be all kinds of people you're likely to meet, S. On any journey that's unavoidable. Like the haughty nobleman who hailed me at a crossroads once. 'Hey Mulla! Which way to the capital?' he shouted out from atop his horse. 'How did you know I was a Mulla?' I asked him, genuinely curious. 'Because I can read your mind,' the nobleman said, when actually he meant—'Because you look like a bumpkin in those rags of yours.' 'Well then, read the way to the capital, sir!' I said and went on my way. Or the time I was wandering along, thinking about dervishes. Dervishes were considered mad only by ordinary folk. Wise men knew that they're actually men of extraordinary perception. Was that true? As luck would have it, just then I saw a man dressed in the robes of the Akldan dervishes, considered a very perceptive group indeed. 'Excuse me,' I said to him, 'please help me understand if you people are as sharp as they say you are.' 'Sure,' said the Akldan dervish. 'Ask me whatever you like.' So I made a gesture with my hand, as if I were grabbing hold of something and concealing it in my fist. 'Tell me, dervish, what have I got in my hand?' 'A black stallion, a golden chariot and a handsome charioteer,' he said at once. 'That's not fair,' I said. 'You saw me picking them up!'

And then there's the question of food. Don Quixote was ready to live on herbs and such, but when Sancho procured fine food for him, he didn't say no. Getting food is always a matter of accident rather than luck, S, especially if the journey is long. Once, around mealtime I decided to catch some tasty-looking ducks that were swimming in a pond. But I'm hopeless at catching stuff, so the ducks flew away, leaving me hungrier than ever. Anyway, I found some old bread in my knapsack, so I took that out, dipped it in the pond and ate it. Someone saw me dipping and eating, and wanted to know what I was doing. 'I'm having some duck soup,' I said. 'Want some?' But once it was even worse. I had absolutely nothing to eat, not even stale bread, and I was sitting by the roadside, dreaming of the meal I would have liked to have—a nice big bowl of my wife's best soup. I could see the bowl in front of me, the steam was rising, the aroma was making my mouth water, the spoon was waiting to be raised to my mouth. I felt madly hungry. I even considered knocking on the door of a little house near the road and asking if they would give supper to a poor fakir, when I noticed a little girl tugging at my sleeve. 'Please sir,' the girl said. 'My mother sent me. Do you have any more of that delicious soup—we're so hungry!' Oops. It seems they had smelled the soup of my dreams!

And once I was looking for eggs in a tree. I thought I'd sell them and use the money to buy some food, or maybe even boil a few to keep me going until I came to a market. A busybody came along and asked me what I was doing. 'Looking for eggs,' I said. 'What, in last year's nest?' 'And why not, you think the birds would have laid their eggs in a new nest, with everyone looking?' I tell you, some people are really stupid, even when they *appear* to be wise. Like this wise man I met who had been meditating for many years in a forest. 'May I join you?' I asked. 'Perhaps I will learn something.' 'By all means, do,' the man said. 'I'm meditating on the oneness of all creatures.' 'Oh?' I said. 'That's interesting. I once had an experience where a fish saved my life—would that count?' 'But that's amazing!' the man said. 'Amazing! You don't need to meditate, you have already *experienced* the oneness of all creatures. Tell me, how did this amazing incident take place? How did you make the fish understand you, how did it know your life was in need of saving, and how, and this is the most important question, how did it save you?' 'Oh it wasn't that complicated, sir,' I said. 'You see I was starving—if I hadn't caught, fried and eaten that fish in time, I would surely have died of hunger.' How livid he got, that wise man. But it was true— that fish saved my life.

'Wonderful,' I said. 'I think I'll write a book now—*Mulla Nasruddin's Guide to Seeing the World.*

'Chapter One: Always carry a good book. MN's recommendation: Don Quixote.

'Chapter Two: How to beat the weather. MN's travel tip: Take off your clothes when it rains.

'Chapter Three: Make friends with fellow-travellers. MN's handy hint: Perform tricks with chariots and horses.

'Chapter Four: Never travel on an empty stomach. MN's

emergency recipe: Imaginary duck soup and invisible eggs.'

You'll get there yet, S, you show every sign of being a worthy Seeker.

And so my wonderfully sarcastic comments were lost. Water off a duck's back. At least no one could tell me I didn't know how, and when, to use my proverbs. Some consolation.

Was it a secret code?

That weekend, I googled Mulla Nasruddin. There were
essays on him and they were all very difficult. I didn't
understand all that stuff. Sufism, the concepts, the meanings,
the path. There was something on one of the pages, though,
that grabbed my eye—a grid with numbers. It looked like a
Sudoku puzzle. And then there were pages that showed
certain letters were equal to certain numbers. And blocks of
letters = certain meanings. The meanings were like 'mother',
'story', 'bird'. It was all very weird. Nothing at all like MN
himself. But I liked the number grid so I copied it down:

4	9	2
3	5	7
8	1	6

And while copying it down I saw that it *was* like a solved

Sudoku puzzle—except here every row and every column (and even every diagonal) added up to 15. Papa used to love doing Sudoku. He was so good at it. Early morning with his tea he would sit and finish off the Sudoku in the paper so Mummy and I never got a chance. Not that I hadn't tried. I was just no good at it. But this! This looked like a magic square. It used all the numbers from 1 to 9. Was it a secret code?

I was determined to crack the secret code, even if I stayed up all night.

One wrong word could mean death

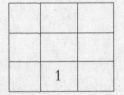

Who knows how long I stared at it before I found myself in a labyrinth. It was a stone labyrinth, the walls thick and strong and made of grey brick. The walls were very high but there was light coming in from the top. But that didn't help much, the light was grey, like the walls, and it was cold. The floor of the labyrinth was made of stone, smooth and slippery like marble, or polished granite. There was something on the floor where I was standing. It looked like a spear. I stepped back (my feet were cold—I had left my slippers behind) and squinted at it. No, it wasn't a spear, it was a letter. I. I? No, it wasn't 'I', it was the number 1! The 1 from the magic grid …

If I cracked the code I would leave the labyrinth, if I didn't I would be stuck here, forever and ever.

Every hair on my arm stood up.

In front of me, half-hidden in that grey light, stood a tall man with one eye in the middle of his forehead. He said nothing. He did nothing. He held nothing in his hands, no sword, no club. As I watched, he crossed his arms, as if barring the way, putting a thick heavy bar, no, *two* thick heavy bars, across a door. And he just looked at me with that one eye and I froze.

Could I run past him? But in which direction? On either side of me there was an opening in the wall. One-eye stood bang in front of me. His arms looked long enough to grab me if I tried to run either left or right. No chance of fighting him. I had nothing, not even a slipper I could take off and throw straight at his eye. I had nothing—except the magic square. I tried to remember the numbers. I stood on 1, which meant 8 was to my left and 6 to my right. But how did I know that for sure? Which way was I facing? Was 8 in front of me, and 6 behind? My head started spinning. I had to get past One-eye, I had to.

'What have I got in my hand?'

The voice was like a girl's. I whirled around thinking someone else was hiding in the half-dark, but no, it was One-eye. He had asked me a question. What have I got in my hand? That was MN's question to the Akldan dervish. Only I was no Akldan dervish. What had One-eye got in his hand? My own hands were sweating. If I got it wrong, I would

never get out. I would be trapped in this horrible cold and
dark, I would never see Mummy again—

'Stop!'

My voice was cracked and shrill in the silence. No one
had moved. One-eye stood like a big stone statue. He was
waiting for my answer. What did he have in his hand? Which
hand, right or left? They were resting on his forearms, big
muscled forearms. Each hand was resting on an arm. Which
meant that what he had in his hand (whether he meant right
or left) was—

'Your arm, sir!' I suddenly found myself saying. 'Your
arms—right and left—which are all the arms you need, sir—
better than rifles or guns or spears. You are armed with strong
arms, sir. You can do armies harm with those arms, sir. Fire-
arms for-hire arms, sir!'

And without thinking-looking-stopping I dashed
through the opening to my right … and found myself safely
in the next square, which was neither 8 nor 6 but 5, and
closed on all three sides, which meant the only way I could
get out of there would be to go back to Square 1 where
One-eye stood, waiting to crush me with those big iron
arms in punishment for the silly nonsense I had babbled
without thinking, without thinking that one wrong word
could mean death.

Get out and get out fast

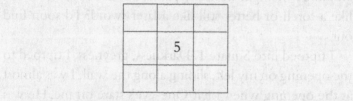

The number 5 square didn't have the number drawn on the ground but the outline of a hand—four fingers and a thumb. For some strange reason I felt like placing my own hand inside the outline. It looked very small and silly and I snatched it back. And when I looked at it, I almost shouted out loud. There was a golden light coming out of it. It looked like I had dipped my hand in some gold paint that made my palm shine. I shook my hand to shake the light off but it wouldn't go. What did this mean? Would my hand fall off? Was it melting? What would Mummy say when she saw me with one golden hand, what would my friends say?

And then I realized I might never see them again.

I had to get out, and get out fast.

Which meant I had to face One-eye again.

Could I blind him with the light? Could it be that simple? I never said it was simple. (MN's words rang so strong in my brain, I almost thought he was standing behind me. No such luck. I was alone.)

I decided to shield my eyes with my hand, palm facing outward and, tiptoeing along the wall, let myself back into Square 1 like a shadow. The first thing One-eye would see would be the light from my palm. Could I focus it at him like a torch or better still like a laser sword? I'd soon find out.

I tiptoed into Square 1. Darkness, greyness. I tiptoed to the opening on my left, sliding along the wall. I was almost at the opening when I felt One-eye's stare on me. He was close, very close and he would stop me any second and his big thick arms would trap me … I shut my eyes, raised my palm and fell backwards through the opening into Square 6, shouting at the top of my voice.

Have you ever had your computer screen turn upside-down?

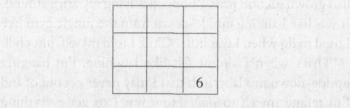

It was only after I stopped shouting that I realized I was safe. Intact. No leg had been pulled off by One-eye, no arm. Nothing, not a scratch. I sat up feeling foolish, and looked at my hand. Where the golden light had been, an ashy grey stain remained. The stain was the same grey as the light that came in from far above. It didn't hurt, but somehow I knew my hand had hurt One-eye badly. Maybe I had burned him. I felt sick. I stood up, and my head spun. The 6 had swung dizzily into a 9. Was I in 9 then? What was going on? Why was it dark suddenly as if I were underground? Why was there a grey mist far below my ... head? My head was swinging emptily in space and my feet were above my head. I was upside-down. The whole square was upside-down. 'How would you like to be buried, Mulla?' someone had asked MN. 'Upside-down,' MN had answered. I was hanging upside-down.

I panicked. I flung my arms about trying to find something I could hang on to. There was nothing.

That awful sick feeling was rising—or falling—towards my throat. First One-eye, then this. I preferred One-eye to this. My feet were slipping, my feet ... my feet were firmly stuck on the floor, which was now the roof. It was as if they had grown suction pads. I stopped waving my arms around. It was like hanging upside-down from the jungle gym like I used to do when I was little. Chill, I told myself, just chill.

That's when I almost felt like laughing. I'm hanging upside-down in a labyrinth that I may never get out of and I'm telling myself to *chill*? How was I to get everything right-side-up again? What magic word would this magic square demand of me?

And then I heard the buzzing.

On the wall, the 9 that was really a 6 began to move! The 6 was not written or drawn—it was *formed* ... out of bees. The bees made a droning sound, which grew louder and louder as they left the wall and flew towards me. The only bees I had ever seen were on a honeybottle label. You could die of bee-sting. I shut my eyes but that made it worse. I felt I was falling and my hands waved madly and the bees sounded louder and meaner. I opened my eyes and saw the bees weren't interested in stinging me—they were still on the wall, only in a different formation. They were trying to tell or show me something.

It was an arrow. The bees had formed an arrow on the wall. But where was the arrow pointing? I looked around and saw that the square had six exits. I would never have known which one to take. Why were the bees helping me? Or was it a trap? Were they purposely showing me the wrong exit? Maybe that's where the rest of the bee-army was waiting. Maybe … I would just have to try it and see. What other choice did I have? And so I tried to walk towards the exit the bee-arrow pointed to.

Have you ever had your computer screen turn upside-down? It happened to me once. I tapped something and the whole screen went upside-down. Trying to shut down took me ten whole minutes. When I thought I had moved the cursor right, it had actually gone left and vice-versa. I went bonkers trying to sort out how to get to the turn-off button. I had to slow down, concentrate, remember that everything was reversed, and then slowly, as if walking through glue (or honey) I got the hang of it. Walking towards the exit was like that, only a zillion times worse. On the computer screen, I didn't have to worry about falling off or being stung by a swarm of bees.

I tried to trust my feet. They hadn't let me down so far, had they? No reason why they should suddenly come loose. I tried to swing my hands normally as if I were walking in a downside-up world. I tried not to think of anything but the exit, the arrow, and every small step, slow and steady, that would take me there. With my whole body and mind, I concentrated on walking across that floor and when I reached the exit, I placed first one foot across and then the next and my head went wildly dizzy again. I was standing upright in the next square.

This guy was a riddler

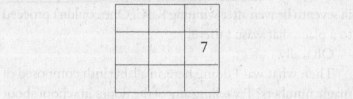

'Hello seventh pilgrim in the seventh year of sadness,' a voice said.

Who was talking? I couldn't see anyone. No signs in this square, no arrows, no people (or person), just this voice echoing around me. What was it harping about? Seventh pilgrim? Did that mean there had been six others before me? And what on earth was 'the seventh year of sadness'?

'Hey!' I said, as the voice rang repeatedly in my ears. 'I hear you!'

'And I see you,' the voice said, multiplied by seven. It wasn't as if seven voices were each repeating the same thing.

It was one voice bouncing off the walls, as if from seven different echo points. I didn't like it at all. If the voice could see me that means it had eyes, that means it had a body and who knew what kind of scary thing *that* might turn out to be. I hoped I never had to see it.

'Shall we, seventh pilgrim?' the voice continued.

'Shall we what?' I said, feeling stupid talking to the walls.

'Shall we proceed to the seventh heaven?'

Was this guy *serious*? Seventh heaven? There was no such thing as a seventh heaven, it was a turn of phrase, an idiom our English teacher liked to see us using. For example: 'She's in seventh heaven after winning KBC.' One couldn't proceed to a place that wasn't there!

Oh really.

Then what was I doing here, in a labyrinth composed of magic numbers? Try telling any of the dopes in school about that.

'And how shall we do that?' I said. 'I mean, proceed—'

'It's easy. Just answer these questions. Your time starts now. What caused the years of sadness?'

What?! A quiz show? The voice must be joking.

The silence in that square was worse than a zillion clocks ticking. The voice was not joking. I didn't know the answer. Tick-tock tick-tock the sound of silence was like a bomb waiting to explode.

'Death!' I blurted out. What else but death could cause years of sadness?

'Yes, seventh pilgrim. Whose?'

Uh–oh. Surely saying 'my father's' would not be the correct answer.

'The one closest to you,' I said, my voice choking at the chance I was taking.

'Close enough, seventh pilgrim. Whose hand struck the blow?'

Why did the voice speak like a storybook? 'Whose hand struck the blow?' Why not simply ask who killed him?

Who? Who killed my father? I had no name no face no person I could pin the death on. It was a bomb. Who made the bomb? Who planted it? Whose fault was it? Who struck the blow?

'The nameless faceless one,' I said, finding it hard to keep my voice steady. We were talking of two separate things, the voice and I. We were on two parallel tracks.

'Perhaps, seventh pilgrim. Who were the six before you?'

'My brothers and sisters in sorrow.' (I could hardly believe my ears. Now *I* was talking like a storybook. Brothers and sisters in sorrow?! Forget in sorrow, I had no brothers and sisters even in real life!)

'Well said, seventh pilgrim. Where were they going?'

'Away.' I had finally blown it. Going 'away' could not be the answer. That was merely what I had wanted to do. Stupid, stupid, stupid.

'What were they seeking?'

'Joy,' I said, suddenly not caring if I was wrong. 'They were going away from sadness towards joy.'

'And what prevented them?'

'The labyrinth,' I said. What else could it be?

There was that dreadful silence again, hurting my ears the way even the voices hadn't. Had I goofed up?

'Hello?' I called. 'Anybody there?' They always said that in movies, just before something dreadful happened.

'Nobody but you,' the voice said. 'And you are free to go, though the freedom is not in the going.'

Huh?

'Does that mean—'

'Yes, you got the answers right,' the voice said, 'insofar as answers can be considered right.'

This guy was a riddler. What was MN always saying about questions and answers? The truth isn't simply the answer to a question. I seemed to have answered the seven questions satisfactorily enough. But what about the 'seventh heaven'? And where were the other six pilgrims? Would I meet them? Had they left a trail I could follow? I had many questions of my own but I was afraid to ask them. And even if I did, would I understand the answers? No, as MN said, some questions are best left unasked.

'What next?' I said, more to myself than in the hope of being answered, but the voice answered—'What's next is what follows.'

What follows? Follows what? Who should I follow? Or was someone following me? I looked over my shoulder and I jumped as if I had been bitten—by a tall wavering shape. Had One-eye followed me? Was he standing beside me now, casting a long shadow in the suddenly-bright light? And then I realized what it was and laughed out loud. I was looking at my own shadow! I was one of those idiots who are terrified of their own shadow. Any other time I would have been ashamed, but now I just wanted to laugh. What follows is always, always, one's shadow, even if you hardly ever notice it. The voice was giving me a clue. I looked over my shoulder again. My shadow was falling over a part of the wall. I took two steps towards it. My shadow moved with me. Wherever I went my shadow would go too. *How would that help?* I felt like kicking the wall. And I *was* kicking the wall where the shadow and I merged into one, only suddenly there was no wall but a door that opened up before me as if the wall had never been there. I was through—

Someone had got there before me. That 'someone' looked exactly like me.

The right door had to be
the right door

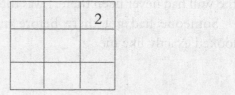

I don't know which of us was more frightened. The other boy yelled and whirled around and so did I and then I couldn't see him. Where had he vanished? My skin crawled. I whirled around again and there he was, looking as if he was going to faint.

'Are you—' we both said at the same time, and stopped, at the same time.

'I'm Shashank,' we both said. 'Are you—'

If it hadn't been so horrifying it would have been hilarious. Anyone who thinks having a twin is fun should get his brains examined. It's terrifying. Especially if you never knew you had one until you were in the middle of a labyrinth you might never get out of.

'Aaaaargh!' we both screamed and ran as if to hit each other. A cold hard surface stopped us from banging into one another and busting our noses.

We both smiled the stupidest, corniest, silliest smile you could ever get to see on a (supposedly) smart boy's face. Twice, not once, but *twice* I had behaved like an absolute idiot. First I didn't recognize my own shadow; second I didn't recognize a mirror until I walked slap-bang into it. MN was right. The word for me *was* dum-dum. Forget Persian rugs, I didn't even know my own reflection. But then I was in good company. What about MN's moon-in-the-well? That thought cheered me up so much, the face in the mirror couldn't have been more different than when I saw it a few minutes ago.

But smiling cheerfully (or bravely) would get me nowhere. This was the room of doubles. Twins. 2. Two sides to every story. Heads and tails. One two, buckle my shoe.

I looked around. Behind me was the mirrored wall from where my 'twin' looked back at me. To my left and right were two identical doors, each marked OUT. Taking the wrong one might lead me back to One-eye. How would I choose? If I were littler I would have done 'inky-pinky-ponky-father-had-a-donkey'. Donkeys! MN's favourite little animals. But no, I couldn't do inky-pinky-ponky, not with my double watching me. Toss a coin? Did I even *have* a coin? I dug into my pockets and there at the bottom, mixed with some torn bits of paper, was a one-rupee coin. Looking at the coin made me feel strange. The coin was so normal, so everyday. I felt the coin came from a world already too far away to be real. I took the coin and tossed it, and as it fell I shouted—'heads-left, tails-right'. It landed tails. So it was the right door for me. The right door had to be the right door.

Right?

Without pausing to wave goodbye to my double, I opened the door on the right-hand side and walked into what looked like a pool ... of blood.

The rain was red

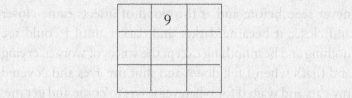

It was raining. But the rain was red. Blood red. I felt it splashing down on me and into the red pool at my feet. I tried to step back through the door but there was no door anymore. Just a hard cold wall behind me. I covered my head with my hands but the thick heavy drops got into my shirt, into my eyes, my mouth. I had to get out of it. I ran and suddenly frogs were jumping all around me. They were slippery and they croaked as I ran, trying to push them off me. It seemed as if I was back in the upside-down square, for the sound around me was of bees buzzing. Larger, angrier, louder bees. They droned and buzzed and as I ran they became smaller and started stinging and biting, making my arms, my legs, my face itch like mad. I scratched and scratched until, as suddenly as they had come, they were gone and all I could hear was the sound of dogs howling. They howled and then stopped. For a second it was quiet and something black was on my arms. I scratched my arms. The black spots turned into boils. I shouted but no one heard me because hard pellets of ice were falling everywhere, hitting the ground with a deafening drumming sound like stones on a tin roof. It turned freezing cold and then boiling hot. A hot wind blew, full of the wings of an insect I had never seen before and as the cloud of insects came closer and closer it became darker and darker until I could see nothing and hear nothing except the voices of women crying and that's when I fell down and shut my eyes and covered my ears and waited for whatever it was to come and get me.

Shouldn't I be a real hero and choose what really frightened me?

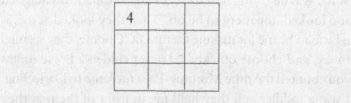

When I woke up, the air was clear and I was lying at a crossroads.

There was no one there but me lying under a tree. It was quiet.

What had I just been through?

What I had just been through wasn't a place—it was a nightmare. Was I still alive, or just dreaming that I was alive? Or was this the 'seventh heaven' and was I, in fact, dead?

I sat up. Four roads were leading off in four different directions. My body still ached from the memory of the previous square. Why couldn't I just go home? Why why why.

I stood up. I almost expected to be knocked down by something, anything, black furry wings, or small buzzy ones, a cloud, a falling tree, a bolt of lightning—anything could come out of the blue in this awful labyrinth.

I had to get out. But how? How?

And then I saw them. Four horses, one on each road, stamping and neighing. One was jet-black, the other snow-white. The third was ruby-red and the fourth peacock-blue. I was seeing things. Trying to make you see things for what they really are. (Why was MN an echo in my brain? What was he trying to tell me?) They stamped and neighed and looked impatient to be off. Then they looked at me, as if I was to blame for making them wait. 'Choose,' they seemed to say, 'and choose quickly.' I'd never ridden a horse unless you counted the time Mummy-Papa took me to Darjeeling. I was a toddler and they held me in front of them as they rode the ponies on the Mall. That didn't count! These horses didn't even have saddles or bridles. And they looked like they could race like the wind …

But I couldn't stand there forever, waiting for a Mercedes to pull up with a chauffeur to take me home. Choose, you idiot.

How would I choose? I guessed that each horse would take me down a different road. But the four roads looked identical. Ok, maybe they looked identical, but surely they led to four different directions. East West North South. The four cardinal points on the compass. I remembered the map-calendar and the beautifully drawn compasses on them, always showing North. Which was north? Which way was home? There was no sun to tell whether it was morning or afternoon. At home, in Bombay, you could tell North–South simply by looking at the direction of the crowded trains. In the mornings, all the crowded trains went south, in the evenings all of them went north. The trains—

I felt great anger. Always the same things coming back to me—trains, bombs, blasts. *Leave me alone*, I wanted to shout, *go away*!

It was only when I saw the horses trotting off that I realized I must have said the words out loud. The horses understood what I said! If they disappeared, so would my chance of getting away.

'No, wait, stop!' I shouted. They stopped and pawed the ground and looked at me accusingly. 'Can't make up your mind, you silly human,' they seemed to say.

'I will, just give me a moment,' I said, almost apologetic, and then I looked at them again carefully. The jet-black horse was proud and stately, fit for a king—or a devil. It looked as if the slightest thing would make it throw off its rider in anger. No, not black.

The white one seemed nice. It was sleek and gentle. Princes always rode white horses in fairytales. This was no fairytale. I hated admitting it but something about the white horse frightened me. It looked too nice, too gentle, too— unreal. Like it was a ghost of a real horse … like it might vanish when I got on its back, leaving only mist …

With a strange sensation of falling through thin air, I tore my gaze away from the white horse and looked at the strangely-coloured ones. The red one was even scarier than the white one. It had blood-red eyes, and the very thought of blood made me sick.

Which left me with the peacock-blue horse. It stood there, looking weird. A blue horse. It was a beautiful blue— the colour of peacock's neck. Our national bird. I had once seen a peacock dance and it was so beautiful. I stepped towards the blue horse.

The blue horse knelt down.

Clumsily, I climbed on its back. It got up smoothly and flicked its mane, which shimmered blue and emerald-green. 'Where to?' the toss of the mane seemed to ask.

Home, I said, in my mind.

The horse didn't move.

Back home.

No movement.

Back home to my mother and my friends.

We stood, as if frozen. I was going to have to figure out a way to get the blue horse to move. Should I dig my heels into its sides? I didn't dare.

'Go down the road,' I said, aloud. 'Go where the road takes you.'

At once, it started trotting, and as I left the crossroads I thought I heard the other horses whinny in a way that sounded so much like human laughter, it made my skin crawl.

We rode for a long time before I saw something familiar ahead of me. I had seen that tree before and those four roads …

I was back where I had started—at the crossroads. There they stood, Jet-black, Snow-white and Ruby-red, looking as if they hadn't stopped laughing.

'But—' I started to say and stopped. I had been tricked. All roads led back to the crossroads. This was the real labyrinth. I would never get out—

The blue horse knelt down. There was nothing else left for me to do. I got off.

I had two choices. Ride the horses one by one, or walk. Three choices. Red, white and black.

Suddenly MN's story about sitting at a crossroads putting in time for something that might happen when he wouldn't be around to see it came back to me. And that other story of a rich man shouting rudely to him at a crossroads, 'Hey Mulla tell me the way to the capital!' To which MN said, 'How did you know I was a Mulla?' And the rich man, who had meant it as an insult, said, 'Because I can read minds.' To which MN said, 'Then read the way to the capital, sir!' and went off, laughing. Oh MN, if only you were here to tell me which road to take!

And then it came to me.

There was one road I hadn't thought of and that was *the road at the top of the tree*. Peacock-blue snickered as if he had overheard my thoughts, but that didn't bother me. What if I *did* find a road up there? Sure, it sounded stupid, as if this was Jack and the Beanstalk or the Magic Faraway Tree, stuff for kids, but MN didn't seem to think so, and MN was a grown and wise man (something I had never admitted before). And anyway, what did I have to lose? Not even my slippers, as my feet were bare. I'd climb the tree and see what happened. Worst case, I'd have to climb back down and try the horses one after the other, hoping one of them would lead me out, which I doubted. So, tree, here I come.

It was an easy tree to climb. Soon I could see sky. Blue, sunny sky. I parted the last leaves, poked my head out and found a wall right next to me. I just had to leap from the tree to the top of the wall and jump down into what looked like a garden, filled with rose bushes and a smell that made my mouth water. I had escaped the crossroads! As I rejoiced at the thought, I heard the faint sound of four sets of hooves galloping away ...

Everything I needed was here

I hadn't realized how hungry I was until I stood in that sunny garden, inhaling the smell of perfectly ripened fruits. My stomach growled. What if I helped myself to one fruit, just one teeny apple or pear? Would the keeper of the garden—for surely such a Garden would have a Keeper to keep little boys out—thrash me if he caught me? I didn't care. I was too hungry and it all smelled too good. Those were water-melons at my feet, big green water-melons among the curling creepers, but I would need a knife to eat one of those. Next to the water-melon patch was a huge tree with clusters of berries. I reached up and plucked one cluster. The juice ran down my bare arm. The berries were sweet but too small to be called food. In fact the taste of the berries made me realize that what I really longed for was real food, something hot and yummy. But that would remain just that—a wish. (If wishes were horses.) For now, an apple or a pear would have to do.

And then I saw them. On a wooden table, three silver platters of fruit. Peaches, plums and pomegranates. They were huge, bigger than the ones I had seen back home, and they attracted me like magnets. I had never eaten peaches and I didn't like pomegranates, but plums were my favourite. I was just about to pick up one shiny purple plum when I noticed something written on the silver platter on which the fruit was arranged. I squinted at it—it said *WOES*. Woes? What an old-fashioned word! Did the other two platters also have words on them? They did. The one with the peaches said *WISHES* and the one with the pomegranates said *TEMPTATIONS*. Woes, wishes, temptations. What?! These were not real fruit but woes, wishes and temptations? Who was cruel enough to make them look and smell like fruit when all they were ... were three *words*? It was cruel and evil and unfair.

I looked at the plums. What kind of woes could plums cause? A stomach-ache maybe, if you ate too many, especially if they were sour. These didn't look sour. But I had been too long in the labyrinth not to know that stomach-aches didn't count for much in a place like this. These woes must be serious woes. Like losing all your money. Or getting a dreadful disease. Or having no family. Or growing old and losing all your teeth. Or dying.

There I was again.

Shashank the Sad. Shashank the Woeful.

Suddenly I didn't feel like eating a plum anymore.

The pomegranates sat sleekly in their skins. Shiny reddish-orangey skins. I disliked pomegranates because the seeds made a pulp in your mouth. Sometimes they were really sweet but I hated chewing them only to get pulp in my mouth. I would spit it all out and Mummy got so mad she stopped buying pomegranates. Why were pomegranates temptations?

Without thinking I took a pomegranate and hit it hard on the side of the wooden table. It split open. I looked at the smashed fruit and suddenly I felt I could stay in this garden all my life. Who needed to go home? Everything I needed was here. I could play and run about and help myself to fruit and perhaps make friends with the Keeper who would take me home and feed me hot meals. No school, no worries, just fun and games. This would be my home. Home, sweet home.

As I spat out the pulp of the seeds I had been chewing without realizing it, I suddenly saw Mummy's face. She was crying. She looked very lonely. I pushed the pomegranate platter away as if it was full of snakes and started trembling. I had almost forgotten about Mummy. I had been thinking only of myself and I had forgotten about her. I had to get out. I had to.

The wishes were my last hope. What would I wish for? Please, wishing-peach, take me home? That wouldn't work, not here. Nothing was easy here, nothing happened the way you thought or hoped it would. Three wishes. In stories it was always three wishes and everyone always chose the wrong three, or said the first three things that came into their heads and wasted their wishes. I knew all that, but so what? What I really wanted would never come true, no matter how many wishing-peaches I wished on. My father would never come back.

And not knowing what to wish for when the only wish I wanted would never come true, I just sat there, till the sun began to go down and the trees began to cast long shadows and the air began to grow cold. The plate of peaches lay in front of me. I picked up a peach and ate it. Then another. Then another. The juice ran down my chin, sweet and thick. The skins were soft and slightly fuzzy under my fingers. I took each seed out of my mouth and looked at it. I held the seed to my ear and heard the tiny sound of something rattling inside it. I sucked each seed clean and then rubbed it on my shirt. Soon I had three seeds on the table in front of me. I picked them up and shook them like dice in my palm. And then, I knew I would have to start leaving. The seeds are mine to keep or throw away, MN had said to his wife. He was right. I put the three seeds in my pocket and looked around.

The garden had vanished.

Start walking

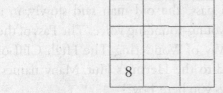

I was standing at the edge of a cliff. I could hear something that sounded like a waterfall. Far below the cliff were little lights. Perhaps they were houses. Cities. My house. My city. My heart leapt.

I was stranded on the edge of a cliff.

The path I was standing on wasn't very wide. Behind me was steep rock. If I called for help, would someone hear me? Here? In this wilderness? There was no one to hear me. My mouth felt dry, as if I hadn't just eaten three deliciously juicy peaches.

There was only one thing to do. Start walking. And so I did, downwards, where the lights lay. I would walk and walk until I reached the lights. Simple.

I had not taken ten steps when I saw someone standing in the middle of the road, looking out at the far-away lights. He was very old, I could tell from the way he stood bent over, with a stick in his hand. I hoped he wouldn't notice me and I could slip past. He was so old—his hair was white, his beard hung to his knees—that he probably couldn't see or hear too well. But the road was too narrow to slip past him. And so I said, 'Excuse me?'

The old man turned old grey eyes on me. At first I thought he must be blind. 'Excuse me, can I pass?' I said loudly. 'Yes, this is a pass,' the old man said slowly, in a surprisingly soft and young-sounding voice. 'The Pass of the Eternal Eight. The Way of Wondering. The High Cliff of the Heart. The Road to the Hermit's Hut. Many names, one road. What brings you here, boy?'

This is what I had dreaded. Old people always like to talk, whether *you* want to or not. Now he wouldn't let me go without asking me many unnecessary questions. I had no choice but to hurry up and answer. 'I'm trying to get out of the labyrinth, sir,' I said. 'Aren't we all?' the old man said and fell asleep (at least that's what it looked like). He stooped heavily over his stick and didn't say a word. I looked at the stick. It wasn't a stick, it was a sword. Both the edges seemed sharp. The handle was made of some sort of green stone. It was carved and had something written on it, but in a strange script. I was holding my breath and leaning forward to examine the writing when he opened his eyes and gave me a very sharp look. 'You are not in the labyrinth,' he said, as if amused at the sight of my face. 'The labyrinth is in you.'

I gaped at him. What was he trying to say? Could I, like, leave? I was getting uncomfortable, standing so close to this old man with sharp eyes and a young voice and a sword that looked like it could make mincemeat of big strong men. 'Yessir,' I said. 'Could I—' and I made a gesture towards the road the old man was blocking. 'Certainly,' the old man said and suddenly the sword was floating in front of my face. 'You can hold it.' I had no desire to hold the sword. But there it was, an inch away from my face. I grabbed the handle. It was heavy, and my wrist almost cracked. I lowered it to the ground and it went easily. I swung it a bit and it swung further than I had intended. 'What's written on the handle, sir?' I asked, suddenly dying to know. 'It's easy to handle if you know how,' the old man said, mishearing me again (or choosing to mishear me). 'Each of the Eternal Eight has used this sword, or one very like it. You'll find their names carved in the jade, boy, if you look.' So that's what the writing was! The names of the Eternal Eight. Who were they? 'But I see you are in a hurry, boy. Everyone always is. Rush rush rush. Go, go. I won't stop you. No one can stop you.' And the sword that I was just beginning to enjoy holding jumped out of my hand into his. I didn't want to leave, not without finding out more. But the old man was already moving past me, moving upwards, and I had no excuse to keep lingering. 'Sir,' I called out to his stooping back. 'What's your name?' But he was moving around a corner and the word that came floating out of the air sounded like 'shien' or 'hsien', I couldn't be sure which.

Feeling vaguely disappointed, I walked down the path. What had he said—'the path of wondering'? Or 'wandering'? Had I left the labyrinth already? I started to run, as if my legs couldn't wait to prove me right, and I ran slap-bang into the belly of a man. I only knew it was a man because of the clothes, the belly was as hard as a pillar. The clothes were dark and greasy, and smelt familiar—a smell of fire and grease and a strange hot drink that burned. I looked up into Timur the Lame's face. I bit my tongue. Timur the Tyrannical. There he was looking down his long thin sharp black moustache at me. 'Har-har-har, if it isn't the brave boy of little brain!' The words seemed awfully loud on the cliff, after the old man's soft young voice. If he wasn't careful, T the T would start an avalanche. I grinned weakly, and said, 'Pleased to meet you, your highness.' 'Your highness? Har-har-har! We are not in court, little-brain, we are wayfarers, fellow-travellers. No highnesses and lownesses here.' Fellow-travellers? I gulped. 'Erm, I'm going home, sir,' I said. 'Home?' The saddest look came into T the T's face. I never knew such a cruel face could look so sad. 'Ah, little-brain, if only I knew what home was.' And he sighed and started walking away. Why was everyone walking away from me? Why didn't they speak properly, and clearly, so I could understand? 'Bye bye, sir,' I called. It sounded silly, as if I was wishing an uncle or a teacher. Why was T the T so sad? Last I had seen him he was hungry and hearty and able to fend off a pack of wolves with a single spear. And now he was shuffling up the path—alone, all by himself, without a spear or a dog or an army or even a bag of that stinking drink.

I felt terribly sorry for him.

'Hello little brother,' a voice said. 'You seem distressed. Tell me, I beseech you, how may I assist you, and alleviate the sorrow that darkens your brow?'

If I had jumped any higher, I would have jumped right off the cliff.

I hadn't seen or heard him coming but right in front of me stood a long thin man with a stick in his hand and a basin on his head. He was sitting on a skinny, stick-like horse. He was looking at me with utter seriousness, and I had trouble believing that all those flowery words had come out of his thin mouth. I didn't even understand some of them!

'But my humblest apologies, brother. I must first make myself known! I am Don Quixote de la Mancha, at your service.' And he raised the stick so quickly and clumsily that it almost knocked me down.

The man was mad! But he was too polite to be rude to, and so I gave a funny bow, and said, 'Shashank the Sad at your service, Don Quixote de la Mancha.' Impressive words are always useful in diplomatic matters, MN had said. (I'd soon see if he was right.)

The man brightened up. (So he *was* right, that MN of mine!) 'But that is a sign from the gods! You call yourself Shashank the Sad, some call me the Knight of the Mournful Countenance. We are brothers, little brother, in a way that can hardly be anything but Divine Providence!'

I felt like laughing but I didn't. Mimicking his slow, strange way of talking I said, 'O Knight, I thank you for your help, but I am all right now. I can manage. I'm on my way home.'

He looked deeply hurt. 'But little brother, I have but one goal from this moment on and that is to put an end to your suffering. My arms are at your disposal, as is the strength of my pure brave heart!' And he waved the stick so fiercely I was almost afraid of him for a second. If only he had appeared when I had to face One-eye or those bees or during that awful nightmare. How could he help me now, on this path that led straight to the lights of home?

'I thank you, O Knight, from the bottom of my humble heart,' I said, 'It is my great good luck to have met someone as brave and kind as you. You are right, I was sad, but now I am better. I have seen others sadder than me, and perhaps all I need to be happy again is to go home. And for that the path lies straight before me, the path of wandering, or wondering, the path to the hermit's hut.' In my desperation, I was simply repeating what the old man had said to me!

Don Quixote de la Mancha brightened again. 'You know the hermit?'

I nodded, lying.

'Another tie that binds us, little brother! Only for that will I let you out of my sight. You will be safe with the hermit, and safety is not to be scoffed at. Go, little brother, and if ever you have need of me, blow on your tin horn and I will ride to your side, no matter where in the perilous world I may be!' And he moved so dangerously close to the outer edge of the path, I panicked at the thought of Don Quixote de la Mancha tumbling down the cliff with his stick-horse and his stick-spear and his kind heart and his fancy words. I hurried past, bowed again, because that seemed more correct than waving, and walked on.

He was mad, but funny too. He had told me to blow on a tin horn when I needed him. I had no tin horn! Laughing to myself, I walked faster, feeling happier, and almost fell over a person stretched out on the road.

It wasn't a person, it was a giant monkey.

'Sorry, sorry,' I said, backing away. Why had I sent kind brave mad Don Quixote de la M away? *Come back!* I felt like yelling. *Come back and help me!*

The giant monkey was getting up. It had something in its hand. Some leaves or grass.

'No need, time to be off anyway,' the giant monkey said. 'Was just so tired, lay down. They need me. Off I go.'

'Where? Who needs you?' I had a sudden suspicion I knew who it was.

'He's dying. If I don't get there before dawn ...'

'Are you ... is that ...' I was unable to speak. I had been told this story so many times when I was little. Hanuman with the mountain in his hand, the mountain with the sanjivani herb.

'Where's the mountain?'

'Oh that,' he sounded very tired. 'That's just those myth-makers. I know the right herb when I see it, but a mountain makes better headlines. See you. Lost too much time.'

And before I could say another word he was gone. I didn't see him jump or leap or fly but one minute he was there, the next he was not. As if he had zapped himself into space.

'Please,' I said to the empty air. 'Please come back.'

I sat down with a heavy thud on the gravelly road. If only he had come when we needed him, Mummy and I. Why didn't gods come for ordinary human beings? What use were all these stories, when real people died and were not brought back to life?

I picked up a stone from the path and hurled it over the cliff. What if I hurled myself off too? Who was to stop me?

'I was like that too.'

'Huh?'

He was young, my age, my height. But everything else about him was different. He had so many scars on his face, on his arms, on his legs ...

'I wanted to die, so I hurled myself into a place from where I couldn't return.'

I looked at him blankly.

'I liked the idea of saving everyone, but especially the idea of saving my father. And so I dashed in and I fought them all, and then I couldn't get out and they killed me.'

'I couldn't save my father.'

'That's no reason for you to die.'

'Why?'

'It won't make you a hero.'

I stood up. I felt like punching him, hard.

'And that's what *you* are, huh—a hero? What's the use—you're dead!'

'Most heroes are.'

I couldn't get away from the boy's stare. He seemed my age but his eyes were much older. He scared me the way Timur hadn't, the way even One-eye hadn't.

'Go away,' I said. 'Leave me alone.'

'That's your problem. You always want to be left alone and then when you're left alone, you feel sorry for yourself. Go back. Make friends. Live.'

'What are you, my grandmother?' I screamed.

'No, merely a friend,' he said calmly. And he went away, slowly, as if each of those old wounds were suddenly hurting him again.

I couldn't see where I was going because I had tears in my eyes. Tears of rage, the way I always felt when I couldn't understand what was going on, the way I had been ever since ...

And then I saw him. Papa. He was smiling, and he had something in his hands—a box. He was wearing a blue shirt and grey pants. He wasn't carrying his briefcase, which meant it was a holiday. There was something in that box for me. He held it out and as I took it he disappeared and I was left holding air.

They hadn't allowed me to see Papa. I knew why. And so I never saw him and that had hurt me more than I could say.

Until now. He had been right there in front of me, smiling, happy that I had seen him at last.

Such things were unreal. Ghost stories.

Papa was not a ghost. He was my father. My friend. I had seen him. Not everything you saw could be explained. Not everything explainable could be seen. A black stallion, a golden chariot and a handsome charioteer. MN had picked them up and the dervish had seen them. Who was to say he hadn't?

I couldn't take another step.

'Hop on, you look like you could use a ride,' a cheery voice said.

I was sick of strangers talking to me as if they'd known me all my life, interrupting my thoughts, bothering me, advising me, quizzing me.

'No I don't,' I said. 'I'm quite capable of walking, thank you.'

'Oh I don't doubt that for a moment,' the cheery voice said. 'But this might be quicker than shank's mare.'

Shank's mare! MN used to say that! I looked up, in spite of myself, and saw a cheery fat man on a white donkey. A stranger.

'Oh he's strong enough to take two. Hop on!'

The voice was so cheerful and comforting that I found myself climbing on to the back of the white donkey. It's not how you travel, S, but why, MN had said. And here I was, travelling on a white donkey, because I wanted to get home. When the donkey started walking, I almost fell off. I clutched the fat man's robe and hung on. It was a silken robe with embroidered green dragons on it and it kept slipping out of my fingers.

'Hang on to my belt,' the cheerful man said.

I saw he was wearing a belt made of some kind of rope. I looped my fingers into the rope and hung on. The fat man kept talking, not expecting me to join in.

'Long road this, been on it a long time. Ten thousand *li* a day, at least. Hungry work. You must be hungry, too. Here.' And he handed me what looked like a piece of bamboo over his shoulder. I wasn't going to chew on a piece of bamboo! But he was going on talking. 'Nothing like a bit of bamboo shoot. Keeps one healthy. Go on, have a bite.' It seemed he had eyes at the back of his head. Suspiciously, I brought the piece of bamboo to my mouth. It smelt nice. Not a jungly smell but a nice baked or barbequed smell. I bit it hard, thinking I'd have to tear at it like sugarcane, but it was soft and it was yummy. 'Nice, wasn't it? Smoked bamboo shoot. I knew you'd like it. It's a matter of taking the first bite. Always the first bite, the first plunge, the first fall that's difficult. After that it's all hunky-dory. But just as you can't trust *everybody*, so also you can't trust all kinds of food! Like when the Emperor was about to kill that deer he'd hunted. Don't, I said to him, it's not a real deer. It's a mirage. The real deer died a thousand years ago. Imagine eating thousand-year old deer meat! Thousand-year eggs are one thing, a delicacy, but ghostly meat is ghastly meat! Ha-ha. Have you ever had bird's-nest? Now *there's* a real treat for you!' I almost thought he was offering me some bird's-nest over his shoulder, but he was merely yakking. Yak-yak-yak—the sound of his voice and the roll of his donkey was soothing and I had been dozing against his shoulder when he suddenly came to a halt, saying, 'This is as far as I go, so hop off!'

I hopped (or rather slid) off. What I saw next was enough to make me think I was going insane. The fat man jumped off his white donkey with surprising agility and folded the donkey into a small white sheet of paper, which he tucked into his cap.

'See you around!' he said cheerily and walked off.

How could he have folded the donkey up? It had been a *real* donkey, white and soft and furry. I remembered its roly-poly stride, its warmth under my legs, lulling me to sleep in step with its master's voice. Was the fat man a magician? Was this a hallucination?

Neither, S. Come on in, the soup's getting cold.

The hermit in the hut

It was him! Friendly MN, in the middle (or was it the end) of the labyrinth. He stood right in front of me. Behind him was a small wooden hut, hanging close to the edge of the cliff. A hut. The hermit in the hut—was MN?! I couldn't believe it. He was the friend Mad de la Mancha had been so happy to know I knew? Had he made Timur soften at the sight of me? Were all the people I had met on this road— and there had been seven, eight counting MN—were they all MN's friends?

Oh stop gaping, S. The flies will get into your gob. Come in and share a bowl. The wife's world-famous soup. The proof of the pudding—you know the saying. Hurry up before I fold you up and put you into my turban!

I stopped gaping and hurried up. The soup was hot. I blew on it and tasted my first spoonful. It was delicious.

The body was missing

What more can I say? That was the last time I met MN. He stopped visiting me in my room, but that's possibly because I wasn't in my room that often. Besides, it was a room in another city. I didn't hate Delhi. I liked it. I didn't feel like I had left Papa behind. I felt I had him with me, always. Mummy was happy, and here's what's funniest, so was I. Things work out weirdly sometimes. Delhi was full of tombs. We went to Agra, Fatehpur Sikri, Ajmer. I visited them all as part of school trips, then later with Mummy, telling her everything I had learnt about them. History suddenly didn't seem so boring. And I remembered MN's story about his own tomb. He told me he was supervising its construction, to make sure they made it exactly as he wanted. Got to have some creative control, S, he had said. After all, I'll go, but the tomb will stay. Can't have people saying I had no taste. And so he supervised the making of the tombstone, the inlay work, the carvings, the inscriptions. Nothing satisfied him until he had personally seen it all being done correctly. Finally it was ready. 'Contractor,' he said, 'it's still not right yet.' 'What's wrong now, Mulla,' grumbled the contractor. 'The body's missing,' said MN.

At the time he had told me this, I had got annoyed and growled at him. To me it had seemed like yet another gloomy story about death and dying. In Delhi I could see the humour of it. He was right. The body *was* missing. I missed him terribly.

Seeing things differently

And since we're on the subject of tombs, one last story before I sign out. Did MN tell me this? I don't know, or rather, I won't say.

It seems MN's tomb had no walls around it, which was unusual. All it had was a strong door with a huge padlock on it. Behind the lock was the tombstone. On the tombstone was a date. 386. Was it a date? Or a number? Or numbers that stood for letters? The scholars decided it was numbers that changed into letters. The letters spelled SHWF. Expanded, that meant, in Arabic, 'seeing' or 'helping a person see'. And so, blind people visited his tomb, rubbed the dust on their eyes and went away, their sight restored.

Honest.

There are different ways of seeing. Seeing things differently.

MN helped me to see that. MN is the reason I came out of that awful phase with all this writing to show for it, instead of merely gloom.

I doubt he'd be impressed though! He had little love for books or book-learning. Once, he wanted to drink some wine (which he was forbidden). He went to a pub and hovered near the door. 'What do you want?' the doorman asked. MN was too embarrassed to say, 'A glass of wine.' Instead, he said, rather feebly, 'Er, just something to do.' 'In that case why hang around here?' the doorman said. 'Shoo! Go home and read a book.' 'Oh,' said MN, unenthusiastically. 'I tried that—once.'

I hope you do, too.